THE EXTENDED SUMMER
OF ANNA AND JEREMY

JENNIFER ANN SHORE

Digital ISBN: 978-1-7326083-3-7

Print ISBN: 978-1-7326083-2-0

For Irene,
for her laugh,
for everything else

1

FALL

"ANNA, WHAT HAPPENED THIS SUMMER?"

Jess's tone suggested this was not the first time she'd asked, but it was the first time I heard it. Or at least, the combination of words finally registered in my brain, which had been preoccupied with thoughts of the sun and sugar — not the cold, crowded high school cafeteria.

I batted away her hand. Her claws, as I affectionately called her nails, were bright orange, still holding onto the hues of summer. She flicked her wrist dramatically, like a fortune teller or something, and let out a small laugh.

Ignoring the undertone of annoyance in her chuckle, I feigned nonchalance, completely enthralled with separating the marshmallows from the cardboard-like pieces in my bowl of Lucky Charms.

"What do you mean?" I asked, rearranging the blue moons next to the red balloons.

It was easy to slip under her scary-accurate intuition

from many states away, but now, I had her full attention. Skepticism surfaced through her pursed lips.

It was only a matter of time before she scratched at my delicately held together facade and got the entire truth, but I really didn't want it to be surrounded by all of these people, so I tried to delay the inevitable.

No one really remembers how Jess and I met. It could have been our moms through the close social circuit of parents in our town, daycare, or some other very practical way — but she was convinced it was fate that intervened, not her dad running away with his secretary, forcing Jess and her mom to relocate to a small rented house in one of the residential communities behind the high school.

Almost all of my free time was spent in her presence, minus the summers when she visited her grandparents in Florida. We'd been so glued to each other's emotions and life events that I swore we could go on a newlywed-style game show and win it all. I knew everything from when she got a new bruise to when she totally bombed a test. She spoke at my great aunt's funeral last year. I was there when she came out to her parents. She held me as I cried after getting dumped at the ice rink in sixth grade. And of course, we always ate lunch together.

All of the tears, the life events, and the ongoing monotony culminated into many things — mostly her ability to create a big, flashing warning in her mind that detected when I strayed from the truth.

I sensed her scrutiny, and I sheepishly met her eyes, ready for the attack. She pulled on her hoop earrings, which simultaneously grossed me out but indicated I was about to get an earful. I tugged my hair down to cover my own.

"I've been gone for almost three months, Anna. Three months! I know I was busy playing card games with the old folks in the middle-of-nowhere and discovering the true meaning of unrequited love, but I sent you a billion texts to please give me some gossip or mail me an object that would cause blunt-force trauma to save me from that ninety-degree humid hellhole. And you know what I got? From my best friend in the whole wide world? A few very boring updates about some stupid fundraiser and your tutoring."

She leaned, pressing her elbows against the gray laminate surface, and I could see the sun freckles peeking through her foundation.

Her jaw ticked, causing me to cower. After all this time, I wasn't immune to her powers of emotional extraction. I once told her she had the potential to intimidate the hell out of an FBI agent or moonlight as a mob boss if she really wanted to.

Her demeanor shifted toward indifferent, and as I watched her casually picking at the bread from her sandwich, I knew I was in trouble.

She rested her chin on her palm. "So I'm just wondering, why Jeremy Blake, you know, the hotshot basketball player, known trouble-maker, and your brother's best friend, is spending his lunch period ignoring Kim Patterson's lips. Which are exceptionally pouty today. Holy shit, I need to ask her what she's using." Her eyes refocused on mine. "Anyway, he's just been staring at the back of your head for the past thirty minutes and brushing off the people who try to talk to him, and I want to know why."

I knew why, of course, but instead of telling her, I shoveled an oversized bite into my mouth and struggled to keep my mouth closed as I slowly chewed.

I'd been ignoring the fact that he sat two tables away since Jess dragged me to this seat, and I fought the urge to turn around and look. It would only make me feel worse than I already did.

Grateful that my thick brown locks shielded me, at least psychologically, I smoothed my hair from root to overgrown end.

"They broke up a while ago," I explained between bites. "Kim Patterson is sweet and patient and kind, but she was too needy and air-headed for Jeremy to want to stay with her long-term."

Jess's eyes narrowed, but her shoulders relaxed ever so slightly, revealing that her interest in this prevailed over her current state of aggression. "Yeah?"

The memory surfaced of Jeremy telling me about his relationship with her, in his casual yet straightforward way of explaining things. I'd overheard enough guys in school brag about who they dated and how they dumped them, even to girls they were currently interested in, out of some macho habit, but not Jeremy. His ability to be honest without a shred of callousness was admirable, and if I was being completely real with myself, it was one of my favorite things about him.

Despite everything, I smiled, remembering his fingertips playing with mine as the scent of breakfast food and freshly baked cookies wafted through the kitchen.

"He said it was one of those situations where people just don't fit together," I recalled from what felt like one-thousand miles away.

"And when did he say this?" Jess asked, casually.

I paused, suddenly losing my appetite.

"This summer," I answered.

I smashed my lips together, a gentle reminder to myself that if I said too much at once, it would all spill out, and so would the tears. I stood up, throwing the remnants of my lunch away, and slowly slid across the bench.

Jess glanced at me, then at Jeremy, then at me again. "And you two were..."

"Talking."

"Talking?" Jess repeated, slowly. "Since when do you talk to Jeremy Blake about that kind of stuff?"

I swallowed, cursing myself for not just telling her everything in a text message or calling her when she landed last night.

The bell rang, an annoying, high-pitched set of dings that went on for too long. It was my new favorite sound.

I jumped up, stealing a carrot from Jess's tray before it met its demise in the garbage can. She shifted her purse on her hip, digging for her compact to check that this morning's lip stain was still in order. She never quite believed me when I told her she looked great, insisting that the opinions of a "natural beauty" didn't belong in conversations about high-end makeup.

I walked slowly, maintaining my focus on Jess rechecking her next class on her printed schedule, as everyone funneled out of the lunchroom. I lost track of Jeremy, a double-edged sword of relief in actively trying to not think about him and his whereabouts for one-second, contrasting the nervousness, and hope, I felt that he'd appear beside me, scooping up my hand in his.

"Look, Anna, you're going to tell me what is going on," Jess said, grabbing my elbow to pick up the pace. "But I have to haul my ass to Trig in the basement."

I merely nodded and set off in the direction of my next class.

"This isn't over," she called from around the corner.

Part of me really hoped she was right.

2

SUMMER

USING my phone as a light source, I gingerly stepped over the empty cups and sleeping forms of my brother's friends.

The living room reeked of beer, sweat, and bad decisions, and I tried not to breathe too much of it in.

I made my way to the thermostat, questioning for the eight-hundredth time why whoever built the house put the thing that controls the comfort of its occupants at the back door, instead of a more convenient place — like right next to my bed.

Cory and I agreed on principle that we should have the air conditioner on. It was June, after all, and my brother was about to host more than thirty people who would spend hours showing off and trying to out-drink each other in our living room.

Even if the outside crept above eighty, fifty-five degrees was a ridiculous, expensive number that he most definitely changed it to after I left. My parents would have a lot of questions when the bill came, and more importantly, I was too cold to sleep.

That said, it was better to be shivering than sleepy when it came to hypothermia, according to the quick search I did last week after I watched "The Day After Tomorrow." It made sense when caught in a New York City library with Jake Gyllenhaal while the next Ice Age began. It was another thing entirely to be wearing four layers in summer, and it was kind of difficult to move around under so much fabric.

I pressed the up arrow until the backlit display read seventy-four then resumed my game of hopscotch around the passed-out party guests.

In the safety of the kitchen, I flipped on the dim lights under the cabinets, giving my eyes time to adjust. Cory's snoring carried through the first floor, and I snickered, knowing how hungover he'd be tomorrow if he couldn't even make it upstairs to his bedroom to sleep.

In a well-practiced routine, I juggled my oversized mug, a large spoon, a random box of cereal, and the milk carton over to the island, careful not to clang the glass against the granite.

"What time is it?"

I jumped, missing the pyramid of Cinnamon Toast Crunch and pouring a generous amount of milk all over the counter, as a half-asleep Jeremy Blake slid the pocket door closed.

"A little bit after four," I answered, wiping up my spill.

I dropped the rag in the sink and pulled myself up on one of the barstools. My house, and every other house in the neighborhood, had a bar, a kitchen table, and a dining room table, always excessively prepared for the big family dinners that came once a year, at most. I almost always ate alone, perched up at the counter or in my room, but every once in a while my parents, Cory, and I would be on the same schedule for a formal sit-down, and Jeremy was a regular guest at those.

He was almost as common of a sight at our house as Jess, and when we were younger, we played games and biked around with our pool towels tied around our necks, pretending we were superheroes. That had to stop when mine got caught in the wheel, and I met the pavement hard, slicing open my knees. The sight of blood made me woozy, and Jeremy pedaled me home, steering with one hand with his other wrapped around my waist, holding me against the handlebars.

When the boys started high school, everything changed.

We'd all felt like siblings growing up, typical rivalries and arguments between us, but we became strangers that year. The wall between mine and Cory's room never felt so solid. They wanted to act more adult-like, I'd guessed, so instead of picking at Jess and I, they focused on getting the attention of girls in their own grade — and the ones above them. And so they kept to themselves while we stayed in my room with endless magazines and nail polish to keep us occupied.

"What kind of cereal is that?"

He yawned, stretching his arms up to reveal a toned abdomen about ten inches away from my face. I tore my eyes away, gulped down bite, and stared at the box.

"Are you incapable of reading on your own?" I asked, tapping on the bright letters.

He laughed, shaking off all remnants of sleep. "I don't think I'm really awake yet," he said, walking over to the pantry.

I took pity on him and grabbed a clean bowl and spoon, setting them both on the side of the counter. He took down multiple boxes at once, taking the time to read their descriptions, and put the ones back I assumed didn't appeal to him.

"My dad won't let us keep the good cereal in the house," he explained, repeating the process. "Too much sugar."

I maneuvered my spoon around to get a scoop of the soggiest pieces.

"Well, to be fair, he has had to fill, like, six cavities for me since eighth grade. I think we're getting to the point where I'm going to have more filling in my mouth than actual teeth."

He set down Reese's Puffs and Cap'n Crunch, sliding his finger over the flaps at the tops. "It really weirds me out how many people tell me about my dad putting his fingers in their mouth."

"Well, I can't say it has been great for me either."

He grabbed the kitchen scissors from the drawer, clipping a neat line to open and pour from the bag, and I watched him as he moved around pretty effortlessly.

I contributed part of it to years of being here, but the truth was, Jeremy could be at home anywhere, making everything seem so easy and uncomplicated. Like when he came with us on vacation to visit my grandparents in

Delaware, by the end of the trip they were sadder to see him go than me.

Jeremy, like Cory, oozed confidence, embodying that athlete persona fairly easily. They were extroverts, always happy to be in the spotlight and showing off, whereas I voluntarily hung back, watching them from the sidelines.

Actually, nothing really showed the stark contrast between our personalities more than this evening, them having a blast with tons of people and me holed up in my bedroom alone.

Worse, Jess didn't pick up when I called.

Jeremy shook a decent-sized portion of both kinds of cereals into the bowl.

"Um, I know you're kind of untrained at this, but you usually just have one at a time."

I looked at him sideways, and he waved me off.

"Better to have my own concoction than that one with the unicorn cat on it."

"Don't knock Caticorn until you've tried it. It's actually pretty good."

"But is it 'meow-gical,' as advertised?"

I nodded. "It's a special edition from Kellogg. They had a plain unicorn cereal that did pretty well, too, and I guess their marketing people wanted to branch out. I think it's doing pretty well, I mean, at least the reviews on Amazon are positive. And kind of funny."

He watched me with interest, and I stopped, unable to discern if he was mocking me.

"Cheers, Anna," he said, a playful smile replacing his sleepy one.

He held out his spoon, and I reluctantly met it with mine.

"So instead of experiencing all the debauchery of high school parties, you've been alone in your room watching TV as usual?"

His tone was curious, not judgmental.

"A movie, technically," I admitted.

"Which one?"

"'Demolition Man.'"

"You know, there are streaming services these days, where you can watch a whole movie without commercial interruptions," he teased, pouring himself more Reese's Puffs to balance out the flavors.

"But there are just too many movies to choose from, and I like the classics that TNT picks for me."

"You think that 'the classics' are bad nineties action movies?"

"Kind of, yeah." I tugged on the strings of my sweatshirt, unable to hold in an honest smile. "They are to me, at least."

"And I thought you were supposed to be the rational one of the family."

He was joking, but he was right.

Cory was the sporadic one, the fun Wright kid, who everyone wanted to befriend. He rarely went without plans on a Saturday night, a casual rotation of girls whose names I could recall if I really tried hard enough.

As his counterpart, I was the boring one. The kind whose summer reading is done a month early, who never gets in trouble, the one who is letting life pass by. A lame high school cliché.

I swirled my spoon in the sugary milk.

"Here, try this," he said, pulling me back to now.

His bowl, honestly, looked like an art project gone wrong. The milk turned brown, with weird floating yellow bits at the top.

"It's disgusting," I coughed, chasing the bite with my own normal, one-flavored choice.

He shrugged. "I like it."

An awkward silence settled between us. Suddenly, I felt bad for being so harsh, but by all appearances, Jeremy was unfazed by it. Maybe that was how he saw me, an abrasive little critic who sometimes was in the same room as him, taking up valuable air and space. Or maybe he just didn't place all of his self-esteem in the little things like I tended to do. Or maybe he didn't think about me at all.

My own neuroticism was my most trusted friend, aside from Jess.

"So, Cory told me you're tutoring and taking another round of SAT prep this summer?"

I nodded up at him. "I just really love school," I said, somewhat sarcastically.

"Do you want to be a teacher or something?"

"Not really."

I drained the rest of the milk, absolutely hating the direction of this conversation. Lately, every single discussion I had with someone meant I got asked some variation of that question, and I grew to resent it. I answered it evenly, only because it was Jeremy.

"I do like learning, and the tutoring is more money than I made at that restaurant job last summer. But I have no idea what I want to do with my life."

He raised an eyebrow. "Not even a general idea?"

"Not all of us can get a full-ride to play basketball."

He settled onto the stool next to mine. "I don't believe I have one of those yet."

"Even if you don't get a scholarship, they still want you on the team. You've basically been training for this since you were born."

He grimaced, pushing his empty bowl forward, and I knew I hit a nerve.

I slowly retreated from the topic. Jeremy and I had an abundance of past memories, some of them tucked away in photo albums, but these days, we were on the surface. We would coexist in the same area for another year or so before he went off to play for some big-name university, and maybe we'd bump into each other after that, when-ever life brought us back home.

We weren't two people who shared the stuff that fell under the "hopes and dreams and deepest fears" category, and it would be weird to pry.

But for some reason, I wanted to change that.

Call it restlessness with my own life or a tiredness-induced inquisitiveness, but I suddenly found myself studying him.

In his current absent-minded state, his forehead rested slightly to the left, on the tip of his fingers, while his right hand drew circles along his bicep. His veins flexed with each movement, and I was surprised to discover that my impulse, which I smothered, was to touch his skin.

He'd changed since the last time I'd looked at him, or maybe I'd been blind and never gave him a second glance. He was just such a constant presence, a perfect addition to our family and the community and every other scenario, that he was always just kind of there.

He did well enough in school, but he was known primarily for his skills on the court, leading our varsity team to the state finals last year, where we all watched a crushing defeat by an all-around better team. Jeremy scored a record-breaking seventy points and got the attention of numerous college scouts.

His natural charisma shined brighter with more people around, and he knew how to use all of that to his advantage, sweet-talking his way out of breaking rules at school, the community pool, the movies, and too many other places to name.

Jeremy could get by on that alone, but he laid it on thick in every circumstance possible, and for the first time, I second-guessed it.

From everything I'd learned from my limited life experience and from watching movies — the heroes and their foes — people don't become that charming for the sake of it. They create false auras for protection, out of necessity, and I was suddenly desperate to understand how he did it and why.

His life seemed easy, cushy even, from the outside, but I knew more about Jeremy and some of his troubles, his dad mostly, than most people did, just by growing up with him. I wondered if he let anyone in deeper than that, and the idea fascinated me.

He brushed his hand against the top of his skull, as if he could sense my close examination. His dark brown hair was the longest I'd seen it recently, and I seriously considered twirling my fingers in the curls at the base of his neck, begging him to open up to me.

I couldn't do that, or rather, I wouldn't. I was too timid and almost predictable at this point.

But could I change that? Why couldn't I have a radical transformation of character in one summer? Just like how Logan Lackney transformed from a tiny, pimply kid into a tall, statuesque ladies man between eighth and ninth grade. I wasn't interested in that type of physical change, though. I wanted to mentally free myself, to be more easy-going, light, and adventurous. More like Jeremy.

One of his long legs casually tapped against mine, and I evaluated my own stance, my spine so stiff after years of my mom nagging me about my posture. I forced myself to slouch, trying to mimic his ease.

I leaned my head on my elbow and sighed, wondering if I was hopeless.

His gaze flickered to mine, and we locked eyes, too long for it to be a passing moment.

"Like what you see?"

I twitched, clanging my spoon against the glass. It was likely dim enough that he couldn't see the redness of my cheeks. I cleared my throat, unsure of how to explain what was running through my mind.

"You were just checking me out," he said, mouth pressing into an even line.

I sucked my bottom lip into my mouth, running my teeth across it. I realized that he was right, it wasn't just that I wanted to be like him, a part of me wondered what it would like to be with someone like him, an experiment to peel back his layers and liken myself to his habits. That was the rational part of my brain, the one that could justify my own thoughts, but the senseless part, the one that I rarely indulged, it was flourishing.

He shook his head, eyes wide, and breathed out the side of his mouth. I watched his lips in fascination, tracing the handle of my spoon around my mouth. He looked at me again and chuckled quietly.

My muscles held rigid, unsure how to function after my brain exploded with the realization of what was right next to me. I stood up, needing some distance. I couldn't recall the last time I felt this alive, aware of every single secret desire within my own body. Suddenly, I was very greedy.

I wrung my hands, multiple times, alleviating some of the nervous energy, but my head spun.

Had Jeremy ever had similar thoughts? Did his heart pound in my presence? Could I possibly only be seen as a pesky younger sister to him? Did he imagine me as I am now, five-foot-six with the slightest of curves, or as a chubby twelve-year-old with a mouth full of braces? Had anything in this realm of possibility ever crossed his mind? But also, was I losing my mind?

He watched me pace, his expression amused, until I stopped to lean against the fridge.

"Jeremy," I said, seriously.

He eyed me, skepticism rampant but obliging me regardless. "Anna."

My mouth tried to form any of the questions swirling around, but instead, I blurted out, "Do you think I'm hot?"

He choked on air, and I forced myself not to react.

Internally, I was a mess, chiding myself for my bluntness and questioning my own sanity.

"You don't think you are?"

I squeezed my nails into my palm. This was the first test, I decided, to be both truthful and detached, like being easygoing was the norm for me.

"No," I said, definitively as I shook my head. "I think I'm attractive enough to get by."

I happened to glance down at my outfit — striped black leggings tucked into fleece bootie slippers, covered by a pair of Cory's old basketball shorts, and an oversized sweatshirt, with a tank top, a short-sleeved shirt, and a long-sleeved shirt underneath it all. I looked like some sort of sloppy cartoon character on laundry day.

"Well, maybe not at this exact moment, but in general, I guess."

He pounded on his chest, clearing out his air passage, and I was impressed at how for once, he was off-center and I was unflappable.

"I just want to know if you do," I pressed effortlessly, finding it way easier than I thought it would be.

Feeling confident, I released my hair from the clip and shook it out, only to catch my reflection in the window. I was going to for casual sexy, but instead, I looked batshit crazy, so I twisted it back up and secured it in a pile on top of my head.

"Where is this coming from?" Jeremy asked, searching my face for answers.

I groaned. "Just answer the question."

"Why the sudden interest in this? You don't seem to ever care about anything."

"You're delaying giving your answer, Jeremy," I pointed out. "But that's not true. I care about the things that matter."

"So you think my opinion matters, then?"

"Just. Answer. The. Question."

He clenched his teeth, something his dad definitely wouldn't approve of, and I watched him work out how to answer me. I'd never seen him struggle before. I wanted to see all of the other things that I'd never seen him do before — things that never occurred to me until that moment.

Jeremy picked up our dishes, intending to wash them by hand in the sink, and I intervened, tossing everything into the dishwasher. I closed the lid and stood up to him, crossing my arms.

"I'm not doing this now, Anna."

I liked this, seeing him a little rattled, knowing I was the one responsible.

"Now?" I stepped up to match every movement, so he'd have no escape unless he physically moved me. And damn, I wanted to know what that felt like. "Does that mean there is another option? I know what your summer plans are, Jeremy, and it involves a lot of time within a five-mile radius of me. So I'll be available whenever you're ready to talk."

He narrowed his eyes at me. "What is with you? Is this some sort of summer project?"

"No," I said, defensively.

I dug my hands into the sides of my hips, ready to defend myself, but then it hit me. This could be my in — the way to explore my current skyrocketing teenage hormones and break some rules, learning right from the master of confidence himself.

"But that is a great idea!"

He rubbed his thumb against his jawline. "I'm not following."

"Look, Jeremy, I had a bit of an epiphany this evening about my somewhat dull life state," I admitted, gesturing around me.

He laughed hollowly. "Did Sylvester Stallone and Wesley Snipes help you with this realization?"

"Don't knock 'Demolition Man.' It's actually a great movie and includes references to Aldous Huxley's 'Brave New World,' which is one of my favorite novels. Did you know that it gets compared to—"

He pretended to fall asleep standing up, jokingly crashing into me.

I pushed him off, holding onto his chest for a little longer than was required. "Jeremy!"

"Right, sorry, you were talking about how thrilling your life is."

I wavered on losing my nerve. "Let me keep it simple. My life is very boring. Your life seems to be not very boring despite our similar upbringings. And I was wondering if you would, perhaps, be interested in spending time with me this summer to help me change that."

He tapped his fingers against the counter. "And that has something to do with me being attracted to you?"

"So you are?" I asked, slightly embarrassed at how hopeful my voice sounded.

"I'm talking in terms of hypotheticals, here, Anna."

My heart dropped, and I tucked a nonexistent piece of

hair behind my ears. "I was just double checking. I mean, I would just want to make sure that, I don't know, you were enjoying spending time with me?" My voice went unnaturally high at the end of that sentence, but I was immensely proud of myself for maintaining eye contact with him.

"Are you asking me to have sex with you?" He smirked, biting his tongue.

No, I wasn't, but his confidence made my knees wobbly.

It was infectious, and I wanted to find that within me somehow. I wanted to be someone completely different for a change. Someone who snuck out late. Someone who tried new things. Someone who took action instead of watching it happen.

I stepped closer to him, gathering all of my courage, and wrapped my arms around his neck. I pulled him down, and he let me.

"I'm not," I whispered, praying that the bold move would cover my nervousness. "But I'm glad that you brought it up."

I pressed my lips against his, and after a second of shock, his body reacted, pulling me into him.

The combination of residual sugar and Jeremy was almost too much to take in. I was out of my own body, screaming obscenities into the void. I had to move. I had to touch him, to move against him, to feel. And I did, overwhelmed with immense urgency to slip my tongue past his lips, to feel someone else, to be with someone else, and I breathed it in.

He slipped a hand up my back, under all my layers, moving against my skin until we were breathless.

"Is this a dream?" His question was asked in earnest, but to be honest, I wondered the same thing.

He kissed me again, full of purpose to prove that it wasn't just a fluke. My hands shook, from lust not nerves, as I hooked my thumbs through his belt loops, pulling him even tighter. This was the easiest, most peaceful feeling in the world, and I couldn't believe it took me so long to do something like this.

He drew back, gasping for air. His eyes were inches from mine, and I searched for any trace of regret or confusion. But I only saw desire.

Someone stirred in the next room, and his eyes snapped to the door, then back to me, running his gaze up and down. The nagging of reality came swiftly, and I was acutely aware, as was he, of the rising sun and the many people sleeping near the windows of the living room.

"Go to bed, Anna," he ordered, suddenly annoyed — at me, or himself, or the people in the house, I wasn't sure.

But the thought of leaving him at this moment seemed impossible. I couldn't imagine my body, let alone my legs that felt about as supportive as jelly, would permit me to leave this spot.

"Are you coming with me?" I asked, deliriously.

His gaze dipped down to my hands, and he let out a pained sigh. "Go to bed and think about what you're asking me because I don't even think you know yet, which is absurd considering how 'overthinking' and 'Anna' are almost synonymous."

The cloudiness around us dissipated as he voiced exactly what I was trying to distance myself from.

"I don't want to think, Jeremy," I admitted, tapping his

chin so he'd look directly at me. "I want to feel. I want to try new things. I want to go to different places. That's the point."

"And you want me to help?"

I nodded.

"Come and find me later, and we can talk about it," he said, releasing me from his hold. "Cory and I have to clean up, and your parents will be home in a few hours."

Practicality prevailed, but not for long, I promised myself. I reached up, catching his lips once more, then ran upstairs, taking the steps two at a time.

3

FALL

IT ALWAYS HAPPENS when it's least expected, that end-of-summer feeling.

I was never really ready to trade in my sunscreen for my gray sweaters, but I was well aware that it was completely out of my control.

Just a week before, I woke up, expecting to stretch my tan arms in the sun rays, only to find the early morning dew blocked the light. That instant chill was a sign of things to come, of change, and I felt helpless.

It was curious, though, that a very frighteningly similar feeling of dread fell over me as I hurried down the narrow hallway toward the science wing, a neat row of classrooms just past the mix of English and other language classes.

My ears perked up, waiting for the bell that would officially mark me late to class, as I picked up my pace.

I'd barely collected myself when Jess and I parted ways, only to realize that Chemistry was next on my schedule, and I groaned.

Science class, in general, wasn't the issue. In fact, I found the straightforwardness of all the theories and chemical compounds very comforting, but this year, Mrs. Blake took over the junior-year curriculum, meaning I'd have to spend the fifth period of every day — and the extra period right after it on Wednesdays — staring at Jeremy's mother, the woman with the same dark brown, almond-shaped eyes.

I pushed down the instinct to fall into a complete panic tailspin, which included spending the next hour in the guidance counselor's office, begging Mr. Reeves to switch me over to Anatomy or Earth Science or anything else. It worked last year when Jess and I pestered him until he changed my classes around so we could eat lunch together. In the end, he and his sweater vests were no match for her persistence, but in a high school career, I was certain that pulling off two little rescheduling miracles was not in the cards for me.

"She's just your parents' friend, your long-time neighbor, a woman you wave hello to at the grocery store," I whispered to myself, tucking my shirt in as I walked. "It'll be an easy day. Just stare at the syllabus and keep your cool."

The late bell chimed, and the forced confidence got stuck in my throat when I entered the classroom.

I adjusted the straps of my backpack, a gray Herschel that my mom surprised me with yesterday, and wished instead she had purchased one of those giant, oversized bags that hikers carried around — at least then I could have used it to hide behind.

I glanced around, double-checking that no one was

aware of my inner turbulence, happy to see everyone lost in conversation about summer break and their weekend plans.

The only open seat in the room was next to Tim Williams, a relatively quiet lanky blond with a nice smile. He and I sat next to each other in freshman English, and luckily, when we were paired up, we split the duties equally, not like one of those situations where one person does all the work and the other texts friends for forty minutes. He'd be a solid lab partner, without issue, but Jeremy, the six-foot-one brunette perched on the black lab table, caused palpitations in my heart.

I gave myself another second to recover, and then I got angry, working myself up to cover up my shredded emotions inside me. I stormed over, and infuriatingly enough, he ignored me.

"Yeah, man, when he struck out, I completely lost it," Tim said, nodding along to whatever Jeremy said. "Pretty insane."

They both babbled on about some baseball game for another ten seconds, and I cleared my throat, failing to interrupt. I pulled the chair out, hitting Jeremy's legs in the process.

"'Sup Anna Banana?" Jeremy said as if we were common acquaintances. "Nice to see you. Can I help you with something?"

His outward demeanor was innocent, his shoulders loose, but his eyes, for me, were ready for a challenge, full of questions and curiosity at what I'd do next.

I didn't take the bait. "You're on my desk," I dead-panned, gesturing to him.

He made a show of pointing at himself, then at the desk, then at the chair, with a confused look, and I rolled my eyes.

"And you're late, Jeremy," called my savior, Mrs. Blake.

She waved goodbye to another teacher and opened her bottom desk drawer, dropping her flowered lunch bag inside before kicking it shut with the point of her five-inch high heel.

"Like mother like son, right?" Jeremy said, rocking back and forth on his palms.

Every set of eyes in the very full classroom bounced between the three of us, and I shrank in my seat.

Mrs. Blake smiled. "But unlike you, my son, I'm a teacher, not a senior in high school. I don't need a late pass."

I squirmed, and Jeremy crossed his arms, suppressing a grin. Whatever he came here to do, he seemed happy with the result.

"Jeremy," she said, a little more harshly this time. "Don't make me give my own son detention on the first day of school."

Waving him out of her sight, she picked up the stack of papers on her desk, dropping two at each table.

He saluted her, as she shut the door, and through the glass window, he had the audacity to wink at me before he sprinted off.

Mrs. Blake cleared her throat and encouraged everyone to turn to the second page of the packet. I flipped my hair down to hang near the side of my face in an effort to hide from everyone's stares, which lessened as she covered all of the project deadlines, dates for homework assignments, and the two exams that would be worth fifty percent of our grade. My suspicion that our seatmates would be our lab partners was confirmed on page five, and I earned a happy nod from Tim.

My eyes glazed over for the rest of the period, jerking up when the bell sounded for the next class. I gathered up my belongings, putting everything in its place inside my backpack.

"Anna, hang back for a moment, would you?" Mrs. Blake asked, taking a seat in her oversized office chair in the back of the room.

Tim shot me an apologetic look, and I waited until everyone filed out to approach her.

Mrs. Blake leaned back in her chair, crossing her legs at her ankles. "So you're the girl who was sneaking in and out of my pool house all summer, then," she guessed, a slight hint of approval in the way she said it.

I couldn't help but laugh, dryly, at how irritated I was that Jeremy disrupted my day like this, bringing personal problems into a school setting, which was exactly what I wanted to avoid, and he knew it.

Mrs. Blake tilted her head to the side, just like Jeremy did in thoughtfulness, and I felt like a deer caught in the headlights.

"My cover is blown," I admitted. "Despite my best efforts, staying under the radar is impossible where your showboating son is concerned."

Her forehead puckered. "But you two aren't together anymore? Is that why he has been moping around?"

I pulled at the straps around my shoulders, imagining her, my mother, and their friends, playing bunco and drinking strong margaritas on Friday nights, talking about whatever answer I gave her. I swallowed, frowning at the thought. I didn't want to be the source of any discussion, no matter how fleeting.

Instead, I deflected. "Does Jeremy even know how to mope? I was under the impression that he just glided around on his own mental parade float, everyone and everything going just the way he wanted it to."

"I think you're the first girl who's ever dumped him," she said, trying her best to suppress a smile.

I willed my expression to mimic the emoji with the line for a mouth, revealing nothing, but my cheeks flushed. She raised her eyebrows, and I kicked the front of my shoe against the back of the other.

"Maybe that's why he's still interested in me," I half-speculated, biting my bottom lip.

She stood up, squaring her shoulders with mine.

I tucked my hands in the back of my jeans, fearing that she was going to try and hold them while she scolded me or something.

But she merely walked me to the door, offering a sad look of understanding. "It's not."

"Yeah," I sighed, swallowing the truth. "It's not."

4

SUMMER

CORY'S SNORING wasn't just loud. It was one of those wet, disgusting sets of noises that ricocheted off of its surroundings, a conductorless symphony that found a new crescendo every twenty-five seconds.

He swore there was no better cure for a hangover, which was still miraculously undetected by my parents, than chugging a large blue slushie and passing out poolside.

I woke up from my own nap to the choppy inhales and rolled to the opposite edge of my lounge chair. I wrinkled my nose, repulsed, as a line of drool threatened to trickle down his face.

My mom hummed, squaring up her bright pink ball cap. "Don't you wish our kids could have been born at this age?"

"If they had slept this much when they were babies, I'd still have my old hairline," my dad chuckled. "Or far less gray hair."

"Speak for yourself, Peter." She took a long sip of her fruity cocktail, tracing her finger along the condensation on the glass. "The salon might as well name the waiting room after me, with all the money I've spent staying a brunette."

He eyed her physique, her "Pilates body," as he affectionately called it, while she adjusted her tank top.

"You'll never be a day over thirty to me, Sharon."

She rolled her eyes. "Cory's closer to that age than I am at this point."

He leaned in, saying something for her ears only, and she turned even more red in the heat.

I watched them smile and officially gave up on my own attempt at sleep. I adjusted the back of my chair to sit upright and tucked my towel between the gaps. I dug in my bag, pulling out a pair of sunglasses, knock-off designer ones left behind in Cory's car, and my favorite reading material, "The New Yorker." I searched for my headphones and practically seethed as I realized Cory borrowed them without asking. They were a tangled mess around him, and I poked his side, hoping he'd roll over, but he didn't even stir.

My mother turned her head toward me. "Honey, don't wake up your brother. He had tough conditioning last night and needs rest to recover."

I was sleep-deprived, and without music to drown out my irritation, I could have ripped her head off. Of course, I didn't.

I bit back my retort, covering for my brother and his friends at the same time — none of their parents knew that "late-night conditioning" was code for "chugging an insane amount of beer and playing ridiculous drinking games." At least, most of his friends. Jeremy was just as an important fixture in the party scene as my brother, but I'd never seen him drunk. Or drink anything, actually, remaining the responsible force who slapped my brother awake to bust out the industrial-grade carpet cleaner.

Cory was on the verge of causing water damage to my headphones, and I stuck my tongue out at him, even though he wasn't conscious to see it. I felt a fraction better from that childish reaction, even more so when I pictured myself drawing a unibrow on his face with a Sharpie.

"Did you see Mark and Alicia just arrived?"

My dad gently elbowed my mom, then waved toward the entrance, beckoning them to join us.

I sat up ungracefully, craning my neck to see if Jeremy trailed behind them, and I was immediately disappointed. I managed a polite wave to Mr. and Mrs. Blake as they greeted my parents, like the old friends they were.

"Hi Alicia," I said, sliding my feet up to give her space to sit. My dad and Mark asked the people on the other side of us to rearrange their spots so we could all sit together.

My mom shook her pointer finger at me. "Don't forget that it's Mrs. Blake at school, Anna." She shifted the contents of the cooler to grab a seltzer, extending it to Alicia, but not before some of the cold drops fell on my leg, making me jump. "We don't want anyone thinking she's pulling favorites in class because you're getting good grades."

"Don't worry, I'll just work toward getting C's this year instead of A's," I offered, sweetly, as an alternative solution.

Alicia laughed, slipping off her dress to reveal a trendy

one-piece suit. "Well, Sharon, I didn't have the pleasure of teaching Cory so you don't know about my tough grading style and no-curve policy on tests, but I'm sure Anna can rise to the challenge without question." She winked at me. "So how was that Annual Small Business Celebration last night?"

She bent down to unbuckle her wedges, her bangle bracelets clinging as she did, and I hid my chipped fingernails, suddenly feeling inelegant in her presence. "Typical dry presentation, or did you get some good networking in?"

"Very successful," my mother beamed. "It was so lovely to meet other people and pick their brains on their business growth strategies. We handed out a ton of business cards, too, thanks again for that idea. I just wish you and Mark would have been there for a night out."

"I considered going without him, but I wasn't sure if that would be appropriate since he's small biz, and I'm not, but you know, dental emergencies take top priority." They both laughed at their own inside joke. "Maybe next time."

"Oh, and I wanted to tell you, I got a few last-minute ideas for the Fourth of July fundraiser." My mom's manner of speaking increased with her excitement. "Do you think a raffle is a good idea, or will it crowd the event to add an extra table?"

In moments like these I really missed Jess, and I shot her a text telling her so.

Alicia patted my leg in gratitude before she made herself comfortable in the now-vacant spot next to my mother, settling under the umbrella.

They were lost in conversation, and taking advantage

of their distraction, I unwound the headphones from my sleeping older brother. I ripped them, a little too aggressively, from his ears, and he yelped.

I moved quickly, pretending like I wasn't the culprit in his surprise, as the foursome laughed at his disheveled state. His hair was plastered in at least fourteen different directions, and the distinct criss-cross pattern of the towel had embedded into his skin.

"Well, good morning, Cory! Welcome to the land of the living."

He blinked his eyes and nodded. "Mrs. Blake," he said, groggily.

I opened the notepad of my phone, where I'd jotted down some ideas of what I could do this summer, adding to it with some far-fetched ones.

"I swear, these boys burn triple the energy they do now than when they were running around in diapers," Alicia said, shaking her head. "Mark was fuming this morning because Jeremy dragged his feet during their eight o'clock jog."

I hovered over to the Spotify app, turning my alternative playlist on shuffle, and leaned back to get comfortable.

Mark used the bottle opener on his keys to flip the cap off a beer, tilting his head across the pool. "Speak of the devil. Here's our son with the concrete feet now, dedicating that precious energy toward goofing off instead of training."

Alicia smacked his arm. "Mark! It's summer. Let him enjoy it."

Jeremy made his grand entrance, flanked by a few

teammates and their female counterparts, breezing past the front desk with a wave, and he started to strip down.

If it were possible to make real-life happen in slow motion with the push of a button, I would have pressed it immediately. Multiple times, until it was at the slowest frame speed per second.

I nearly melted when Jeremy removed his shirt, something I'd probably seen hundreds of times before but never paid attention to. I cursed when Cory stood up to join them and ruined my view.

They slapped hands in greeting, Cory making some sort of joke to the group. Jeremy laughed and brought his hand up to his eyes, shielding the sun as he scanned the area.

His eyes met mine, and I held my breath. He tilted his head sideways, waiting for a reaction from me. Both our moms waved and called his name, and I moved my magazine up toward my face, watching him from above the pages.

His brow furrowed, but he was soon distracted by the wrestling match at the edge of the pool. One of his friends, Mike or Matt or maybe Mitch was his name, locked his arm around Jeremy's neck, threatening to toss him in.

The lifeguards whistled, and the entire group fell as a massive pile into the shallow water. Our parents laughed, thoroughly entertained by their antics.

The girls shrieked at getting wet from the giant wave, and I decided out of everything around me, I could channel my annoyance toward them. Jess was a total girly girl, through and through, but these girls were reacting to the water as I'd expect someone to react to splashes of bleach. I was under the impression that people came to the pool to swim and maybe tan, but theirs were fake enough to border on orange.

Kim Patterson and her permanent pout led the group of girls over to a set of vacant chairs, staging their area and making a show of oiling their skin. From my vantage point, I was pretty sure they were all in full faces of makeup, hair curled and styled. Kim dropped the bottle of tanning oil, "accidentally," and made a show of slowly bending down to pick it up, right in Jeremy's eye line.

Somehow, I had transported from a quiet afternoon with my parents into a rap video.

One of the boys whooped as they laid down in unison on their stomachs, untying the straps behind their backs to avoid the tan line.

They were so desperate for attention.

Screw that, I decided, because so was I.

My bathing suit was more fabric than straps, unlike the other girls' ones, but I still double checked the buckles — because that's not the kind of showing off I wanted to do — and threw down my belongings.

"Do you need cash for the snack bar?"

"No, thanks, Mom," I said, standing up to stretch. "I think I'm going to jump in."

Her eyes flashed in surprise. "Finally putting that decade of lessons to good use. She was such a beautiful swimmer wasn't she, Peter?"

"An even better diver," he said, handing Mark another beer before launching into the story, one he'd probably told one-hundred times before, of my failed history with organized sports.

I walked slowly over to the deepest end of the pool, where the diving board and platform stood.

I'd always taken to water naturally, crediting those infant swimming lessons that I'd seen on our home movies. My parents gushed about how much I enjoyed splashing around, but watching it with my own, non-baby eyes, it seemed like a very dangerous version of that cover of Nirvana's Nevermind album.

Still, I endured years of private lessons, perfecting strokes and thrashing to make it across the pool as the coach stood at the end with a stopwatch. I was good, but I never wanted to join the team at school — too many early and late practices and most of all, heated competition. I fled from that sort of thing.

But then I watched one of the Summer Olympics, in equal parts fascination and terror, as the divers, and their bodies sculpted from marble, flipped off from various heights to roaring applause. The fanfare was fun to see, but what drew me in was the serenity on their faces as they readied themselves for the moment they'd raise their arms and dive.

I'd begged my parents to let me try it, campaigning for months until they agreed, and I loved it, the panic, the dedication, the exhilaration that went along with it.

But, as my neuroticism would have it, the night before I was supposed to debut at a competition, I watched dozens of YouTube videos of divers hitting their head off of the board. I promptly retired before I really even started.

I climbed the ladder, breath shaky.

From the ground, this height seemed a little intimidating, but from ten feet up, I could have passed out looking at the bottom of the pool.

A sense of familiarity crept up as my toes met the ragged surface, coated with a special non-slip material. I'd long forgotten the technical names for all the rotations and positions, voluntarily purging them from my brain when I quit, but I knew what I wanted to do at that moment.

My surroundings were quiet, and I felt the weight of everyone's gaze on me.

No one really spent time up here, choosing to splash off the standard diving board at the pool's edge instead. It was an uncomfortable feeling, being watched, but that's exactly why I was up here. It wasn't on my little list, to reignite my diving career, but I promised myself I'd give into challenges this summer, to do things that made me feel a little uncomfortable, for nothing but a moment of gratification.

I stretched my arms up and back, bending down to touch my toes. I bounced over to the edge, and I glanced down, reimagining all the times I had nightmares about slamming my head against the bottom, which didn't make any sense. I could do it, but I couldn't watch it.

I turned around, and Jeremy hollered for me. I looked at him over my shoulder, and Cory, surprised, joined in on the cheering.

"It's now or never," I said to myself. "I'm doing this."

I closed my eyes, centering my mind, and gently started to flex my feet. The bounce reverberated upward into my stomach, and my heart.

Before I lost my nerve, I brought my hands up and

made the leap. I knew how to push myself out without losing my center of gravity. My coach's voice screamed in my head, and I tuned it out, torquing through one, two somersaults then extending my legs, meeting the water with a minimal splash.

My execution was flawless, and I screamed with excitement underwater. Surrounded in a frenzy of bubbles, I fist pumped until I ran out of air.

Everything in me wanted to ride the wave of endorphins, but I couldn't come out celebrating myself. I'd look like a self-serving fool, which I secretly was. I had to swim to the surface, get out of the pool, and act like it was no big deal, like I didn't do that to prove myself to anyone.

I kicked my legs up and surfaced, greedily inhaling the fresh air, just as the group of Cory and his friends tackled me in the deep end.

They congratulated me in fits, begging me to teach them how to do it. I shook my head, but that didn't stop most of them from jumping out to rush over to the low diving board. I pushed my palms against the concrete, lifting myself out off the edge.

Jeremy watched me, treading water on the other side of the pool, and I grinned, briefly, at him.

My parents gushed, and I waved them off, assuring that it was nothing. In one smooth motion, I lowered the back to my chair and laid face down, falling into the most peaceful nap.

The sounds of splashing and laughter pulled me back out, and when I woke completely, overheated but satisfied, Jeremy had taken up residence in Cory's chair. I glanced down to make sure I hadn't revealed anything in my sleep, and to my relief, I was fine, cocooned in my towel.

I ran a hand over my face and through my hair, a tangled, semi-dried mess.

"Hey," I said, quietly.

He turned to face me, propping himself up on his elbow, and a slow smile spread. Water droplets covered his body, distracting me for a moment, and he dipped his head down, catching my gaze.

"Well, it's later, and I found you," I pointed out.

Jeremy glanced over my head, assuring our parents were preoccupied. "You cheated," he said, seriously. "You can't do something like such a badass and expect a guy not to crawl on his knees in your presence. I'm only human, after all."

"I didn't do it for you," I explained. "I did it for myself."

He bit his lip. "Oh, I know. Why do you think it was so hot?"

"You do think I'm hot, then?" I teased him, pulling my towel a little more, as if he could see right through me and how nervous I felt.

"I didn't exactly say that, did I?"

I rolled my eyes and sat up, leaning over to get us each a bottle of water, mostly because it was the hottest part of the day but also because I needed a second to come up with something else to say.

I took a gulp and fished my phone from under the chair. "I started a list," I said, unlocking and handing it over.

His eyes moved quickly down the screen. "Some of

these are a lot, Anna," he laughed. "Get a tattoo? You're not even eighteen."

"Neither are you," I deflected, well aware that didn't help the situation.

"Maybe Cory will take us both."

We glanced over at my brother, who was wearing a set of snorkeling goggles in the kid pool. He blew water through the tube, spraying a group of little kids, making them laugh.

"Or maybe not."

Jeremy locked my phone and handed it back to me, grazing my thumb with his during the exchange. "How about you let me plan something else for tonight?"

I moved an inch closer to him. "Something not on the list?"

"That's going to be the first thing we're going to do to change your style, Anna. We're going to revolt against the list."

"Oh, how dangerous," I mocked. "I'm in."

"I'll pick you up at nine o'clock."

"Oh, um, that's kind of on the late side, isn't it?"

He laughed, dryly, twisting the plastic water cap in his hand. "I'm sure you can watch 'Broken Arrow' another night."

"Fine," I breathed, leaning back with my arms over my head. "And so my own form of 'late-night conditioning' officially begins."

"Hey Jeremy, what do you think about helping out at the fundraiser?" Alicia asked, oblivious to what she was interrupting.

"I think that's a lovely idea," my mom chimed in, practically making heart eyes at Jeremy. "Maybe you could help us with setting up or lighting off some of the fireworks."

"No way in hell is he getting his hands near those," Mark said, gruffly, taking a deep swig of his beer, and my eyes flickered to all the empty bottles at his feet. "Too valuable."

"Maybe Anna will help with the fireworks," Jeremy volunteered innocently. "Her hands will never make it to the NBA."

My dad looked at me. "Anna hates fireworks."

"What kind of person hates fireworks?" Jeremy asked.

"I don't like them," I said, playing with the ends of my hair. "I think they're dangerous, and honestly, a little childish."

Jeremy leaned over, speaking softly. "Low blow, Anna, siding with my dad. I'll have to get you back for that." He pretended to have a mad scientist look about him, folding his hands up in front of his face. "Maybe I'll put them at the top of the non-list list."

I put on my sunglasses, pretending to be completely unbothered by the idea. "The only thing more juvenile than fireworks is you, Jeremy Blake."

"Maybe so," he said, settling in beside me, "but I'm all you've got."

He wasn't wrong.

5

SUMMER

"This is kind of weird, isn't it?" I asked when we turned out of our neighborhood.

I traced the leather seam on the seat, expertly stitched in an alternating pattern.

Even with the windows cracked, Jeremy's presence filled the entire car, pressing against my chest in a more pronounced way than the seat belt did.

When I drove, it was in a jumpy, slightly terrified way, with both hands clutching the steering wheel as if my life depended on it. Comparatively, he drove with one hand relaxed over it, his wrist mostly controlling our direction, with the other on the center console, casually adjusting the settings on the touch screen between us.

After a minute of contemplation, he nodded. "Yeah, I guess. I mean, we have known each other forever, but going from childhood memories to groping each other in your kitchen is a big jump to process all at once."

I broke out into a fit of laughter, and he arched an

eyebrow. "I actually just meant me being in your car, but yeah, kind of on all the rest, too."

"You've never been in my car?' He thought about it, eyebrows pinched. "Wow, you're right." He settled on a hip hop station and drummed along with the beat on his chino-covered thigh. "When's the last time you were at my house?"

I liked to think my parents' house was cozy. Nice, but lived in, with pictures of us covering the walls and tick marks in the kitchen with all of our heights. I could point out the memory associated with almost every scuff on the floor, and to me, it felt like what a family home should feel like.

But Jeremy's was a magazine-worthy structure at the top of the hill, updated in the latest modern appliances in the most minimalist chic way. His parents seemed to have endless disposable income, based on the amount of redecorating that occurred over the years.

I've caught a few jealous neighbors peeking out their windows to see which furniture company was bringing new items up to them.

Whenever I was at this house, which was sparingly over the years, I kept my hands to myself, afraid to mess anything up.

"It's been a while," I said, remembering how Alicia planned a surprise birthday party for Mark, only to have him show up late and smelling of whiskey. "At least, not since you moved to the pool house."

He nodded, lips curling up. "My sophomore year. My mom likes to say now that it was a gift to me, to have my own space, but I can't help by laugh when I picture her face, so angry when Cory and I broke some ugly vase, and she kicked me out to the back."

"Wait a second, why do you guys go to the community pool if you have one in your backyard?"

"My dad fell into the pool one night while sleepwalking. He woke up inhaling water, and I screamed for my mom to call an ambulance. It was scary as hell."

"I slept right through the sirens," I admitted. "My parents told me what happened the next day."

"Ever since then it has been drained and covered. He insists that if it could happen to him, it could happen to me. Can't let anything happen to the 'precious goods,' as he likes to say."

I leaned forward in mock concern. "It must be such a struggle to have all of these people who make you feel so important all the time," I said, laying it on thick. "It's a wonder your head isn't twice the size."

"That's why I hang out at your house so much. My fans keep me grounded."

I shook my head, fiddling with the frayed denim on my skirt.

"If we're being honest with each other, and I think that's what we're doing, that's not the only reason," he cleared his throat, eyes dead ahead. "Even before that, I made a big fuss about not having a diving board, but we couldn't fit it in the 'design aesthetic' or some shit."

"But you don't like to dive," I said, my voice dropped a bit as I realized what he'd implied, and I repeated myself slowly. "You don't dive, Jeremy."

He turned to face me, and I nearly gasped at the vulnerability of his expression. "Seeing you today was amazing, for many reasons, but selfishly, it took me back to a much happier time. Remember that summer our parents finally let us go to the pool by ourselves, on the promise that we'd reapply sunscreen every hour and stay in the shallow end?"

"And instead I almost pulled a muscle practicing my back dives over and over again."

"Until the lifeguard realized no one was there supervising us."

"And the manager drove us home."

We laughed in unison.

"Grounded for a week," he recalled. "But they gave up after a few days."

The memory settled between us, and he turned into a strip mall parking lot. I'd been so lost in my time with him I hadn't even paid attention to the road. "Where are we going?" I asked, glancing around.

"Here," he said simply, gesturing to the bright green lights of the dollar store just ahead.

"And we're going to do what exactly? Shop for bargain beach toys?"

We strolled through the empty parking lot, occasionally brushing up against each other. The gentle breeze cut through the humid air, blowing a plastic bag and empty cups across our path, and despite the homely setting, Jeremy appeared to be immensely proud of himself.

"I was doing some research, and apparently, you can sometimes find discontinued cereals at dollar stores and random hole-in-the-wall grocery stores. I thought we'd try our luck at a few and then swing by a legitimate grocery store to grab some milk and stuff."

I imagined him putting the time into plotting out our route and thinking about me, and I'd never felt so giddy in my entire life. I threw my arms around his neck, knocking him off balance. My stomach fluttered when he put his hands on my waist, and to recover, I grabbed his hand and practically skipped into the store.

"This is like Christmas!" I giggled, moving quickly between the aisles to find the right one.

He grinned, feeding off of my excitement. I shivered, because of him and because of the overuse of air conditioner, which hit the skin exposed by my off-the-shoulder shirt.

I jogged down the row, grateful I'd thrown on a pair of slip-on sneakers instead of flip flops.

The peeling, slippery floors, the yellowing shelves, and abundant orange stickers set the perfect scenery to lead me to the promised land. In this case, it was a shelf full of Franken Berry cereal.

"No, I take that back, this is like Halloween!" I said, grabbing a box and hugging it. "Jeremy, they only have this cereal and Count Chocula available seasonally, and that's only sometimes in October. If you're lucky."

I babbled on about the differences between General Mills, Quaker, and Kellogg, as we made our way through checkout and back to his car.

"I know you're obsessed with the stuff, but I didn't realize there was so much to learn about cereal," he admitted, humoring me.

I set the box very carefully down on the back seat and buckled my seatbelt. "Do you ever wish you could trade all of the random knowledge about a topic for something actually useful?"

"Yeah, but not in this case," he said, punching the next destination into Google Maps. "I see this as a very practical hobby. I mean, if you think about it, cereal is kind of our thing now."

"It's not our thing," I insisted. "It's my thing. It has always been my thing, and you've just inserted yourself into it."

"That's what she said."

I tucked my hair behind my ears, stifling a laugh. "Didn't that stop being funny, like, five years ago?"

"That joke is never not funny."

I shook my head.

"Maybe not as charming, in your mind, as 'the classics,' but I think 'The Office' deserves recognition. It's the perfect show."

We argued about it, how it is funny but definitely did not age well, and talked through our other favorite shows and movies. We kept it flirty and easy in the hour and a half it took us to hit up three more stores, eventually settling in the parking lot of a chain that was open twenty-four hours.

My legs dangled off the bumper of his car, and although he was annoyed that his dad made him drive last year's safest SUV on the market, the extra headroom and space in the trunk were perfect for this adventure.

"So what's it going to be?" Jeremy asked, handing me a paper bowl and plastic spoon from the grocery bag. "Franken Berry or Sour Patch Kids cereal?"

"The Sour Patch Kids one kind of freaks me out, to be

honest. I'm going to start with Nutter Butter then maybe switch to Cinnamon Toast Crunch Churros."

He leaned over, concentrating on pouring the perfect amount of milk, and I laughed at the slow movement.

"Very gentlemanly," I said, admiring his handiwork. "Thank you."

He sat down next to me. "I know I already made fun of you for this, but how the hell do you eat so much processed sugar all the time?"

"Well, sometimes I add a banana to it," I admitted, half-interested in the peanut butter cookies floating around in milk. "My theory is that it makes it at least ten percent healthier."

He pretended to stand. "Well if we're talking such a high percentage, I'll go back in and buy a bunch right now."

"No," I said, too forcefully for the moment to pass by lightly.

"You seem to have a strong desire to stop me from making sure you get at least some nutrition."

"Nope." I pretended to be neutral, but he saw through the act.

"You're lying."

"No."

"Then why are you smiling?"

"Okay! Fine." I put down my bowl. "You have to promise you won't tease me for this."

He put his hand on his chest, like I'd asked a southern, church-going woman to rob a bank. "I cannot promise such things."

"Jeremy."

"At least I'm honest about it," he said, taking a bite and wiping the corner of his mouth with the back of his hand.

"Jeremy!" I insisted. "Promise me."

"I promise to do the best I can. That's all I've got."

I studied him for a moment. "The truth is, I avoid eating bananas in public at all costs."

"Since it's a phallic food?"

"What is wrong with you?" I demanded. "No!"

"I wouldn't mind seeing you eat a banana," he said, staring off into the distance. "Maybe a bag of lollipops, too. A popsicle. I could live with a hot dog. I guess. Kind of weird, actually. I take that one back. Something about the biting and the bun puts me off on that one."

I glared at him.

"Oh, sorry, forgot you were here."

"The real reason is that I barely was able to convince my parents to stop calling me 'Anna Banana' when I was a kid, and I fear the nickname will resurface if I associate myself too closely."

"Well, that's stupid."

"Well, you're stupid," I defended lamely. "Nicknames stick. For life, sometimes. And the psychological damage can carry on for decades."

He spooned up the rest of his milk. "Don't you remember my nickname growing up?"

"Baby Blake," I recalled. "But that doesn't even really count. That name faded the millisecond your cheeks didn't look like frisbees. Besides, you're, like, six-foot-seven-thousand now."

"Six-foot-one," he corrected, stretching his legs. "And my dad had a late growth spurt his freshman year of college. I could be six-foot-five in two years, you never know."

"I can't see that happening."

"Of course you can't see it, Anna. It's genetics. Again, you're supposed to be the brains of the family."

"Let's bet on it," I said, feeling fiery. "If in two years, you're six-foot-five, I'll..."

"Do the flip thing you did in the pool again."

"Okay," I agreed, surprised that was all he wanted to negotiate for his terms.

"Naked."

I scoffed. "You're insane."

"Is that an agreement I hear?"

His eyes flashed, and I ignored him.

"What do I get if I win?"

He leaned in. "What do you want?"

I dramatically tapped my fingers on my lips, postulating on what I could get him to agree to. "Did you know that Kellogg has a store in New York City?"

"Screw the bet, we should go now."

My heart leapt, but common sense grounded me. "It's like a nine-hour drive."

"Good thing we're right next to a gas station, then." He pointed over his shoulder, where the neon sign of advertisements and fuel prices illuminated the storefront and drive-through car wash. "I'll even let you pick the music."

I seriously considered it, imagining us together alone for that long in a place I'd only dreamed about seeing.

Jess and I had always talked about taking a girls' trip up to the city with our moms, but it was always mentioned as something that would happen in the future when reality and money no longer hindered it. She wanted to live there some day, but I just wanted to see it with her, tagging along as she dragged me from store to store.

Experiencing it with Jeremy would be completely different. I imagined us strolling through the city holding hands, eating romantic dinners at restaurants, and discovering how actual New Yorkers lived, not just doing the touristy crap.

It felt like a real possibility now, something that could actually happen, with my dedication to new experiences.

"You and I disappearing in the night, high-tailing it across the state," I tested the idea by saying it aloud. "I'm sure our parents would love waking up to that plan already in motion."

He rubbed the back of his neck. "Actually, I'm pretty sure they would. My mom has always loved you, and well, it's obvious your family would trade you and Cory for me."

I smacked him lightly on the leg, pulling my hand back, but deep down, I wanted to leave it there, and he knew it.

I looked up at him, turning the conversation in a serious direction. "We haven't really spent any time together since we were kids, Jeremy. They'd all be very confused as to why you and I would have taken off alone."

"No, they'd be thrilled," he insisted. "Honestly. Think about it, our moms would start planning a wedding immediately, scoping out potential starter homes for us, and writing a list of names for their grandchildren."

He was kidding, but the reality of the situation hit me square across the face.

The ease of being in his presence evaporated, like my spine got snapped back by a rubber band.

I hadn't considered how my actions, intended to be fleeting, were somewhat permanent. Our parents were close, sure, but Jeremy was a fixture in my family, with my brother especially, and I worried I started something in the kitchen that could change our entire dynamic and couldn't be undone.

"Well, we'd have to explain that it's just for a summer, and that's the entire point of this," I sputtered out, slightly panicking. "Living for a season with no lists, no promises, no rules."

If he caught onto my inner turmoil, he didn't let it show. "Promises are okay. Rules, maybe. No lists, for sure."

"Jeremy, this is supposed to be a summer-only agreement," I swallowed, hopping down to toss our bowls in the trash. "It needs to be."

He tucked the bags into their boxes and shut the trunk door. "You don't think there will be anything that happens this summer that you'll want to carry over into fall?"

I turned to face him head-on, his easy-going posture, his curious eyes, his familiarity, and I inhaled.

"No," I answered, timidly.

"All right, then," Jeremy said, no trace of emotion. "Let's get you home."

6

SUMMER

I TOSSED my SAT prep book aside, and it fell to the floor with a loud thump.

The words were fuzzy as I tried to work my way through a practice test, but my attention span was drained from the back-to-back tutoring sessions this morning.

It was better than running around and collecting people's dirty dishes at the noodle restaurant like I did last summer, but the mental drain was a different beast than physical tiredness. The last session of the day, with a bratty pre-teen, required every ounce of patience I had, and I needed to unwind.

It was my own fault, really, as I was the one who planned such a grueling schedule.

Despite the glorious flexibility of online-based income, I found myself overwhelmed with their needs, especially when I thought about how helping a kid learn to read or solve a problem with simple subtraction could have a profound impact on their lives — and I felt inadequate. I was sure most parents saw it as an hour or two they got back for themselves, low-cost babysitting, with the supervisor keeping them glued to the computer, but I liked to think of it as a little more than that.

As the weeks carried on, their interest all but evaporated, and I struggled to hold onto mine as well.

The kids I hand-picked for their gentle demeanors began to get frustrated easily, combative even. It was clear that they would have much rather been playing in the sprinklers instead of practicing spelling words for a test that had no real consequence on any grading system. It wouldn't be my first choice at their age, either, so I didn't get too worked up about it.

However, it wasn't lost on me that these kids, of varying ages, likely had a horde of activities, friends, and endless entertainment waiting for them the moment our time ended, and all I had was an empty house.

I put away my computer and focused my energy on tidying my room, even dragging the vacuum upstairs to swipe it across my carpet — all of which took me about ten minutes from start to finish.

Jess didn't pick up when I called, even though when she left for Florida, we'd both promised we'd talk every day.

"Don't forget, misery loves company, Anna," she'd said, laughing as we both brushed our tears away. Her mom honked the horn to take her to the airport, yelling about traffic and lines and whatnot.

I'd pulled her into a hug. "We can be bored together from thousands of miles away," I promised. "It'll be a perfect summer break."

She sighed, picking up the last of her bags. "Well, I'm going to try and do something different this summer, change it up. Maybe get some blonde highlights or something to start our junior year as a new, shiny person."

"You think blonde highlights are the key to you being a new shiny person?"

"Maybe," she said, shrugging.

I'd walked her down to the car, and before she pulled away, she rolled down the window for one final word. "And maybe you'll be totally different the next time I see you, too!" We both smiled, knowing that wouldn't happen.

Only now I wasn't so sure.

I scrolled through my messages, down past Jess's name, my parents, our family group text, Cory, a cousin I texted with about every six months, a girl I worked with last summer, and finally, my finger stopped on Jeremy's little chatbox.

Ignoring how pathetic my contact list was, I opened up our history, unsurprised to see my last text from him was actually Cory asking me to tell Mom and Dad his phone died and that he'd be home soon.

That text woke me up when it came through originally, as I'd zonked out on the floor in front of my TV with my phone in my hand, and it had the same impact on me now, rousing my senses from a comatose state of life.

It was definitely up to me to initiate a conversation with Jeremy, after that silent ride home the other night. He seemed lost in thought, while I was painfully aware of each passing second, desperate to know what was crossing his mind but too afraid to ask. I'd hopped down from the passenger seat, mumbling thanks, and headed inside without a second glance.

My fingers moved, typing a message, making the first move — a thing I didn't really ever do in my real life, but this summer was making me change my habits.

I hit send without another thought.

What are you doing?

I cringed, realizing it was probably too aggressive.

At least I was to the point, maybe that'd win some appreciation points. Talking to him in person flowed so easily, and I could play off of his emotions, reading his reaction from his body language. His eyes and lips gave so much away to me, and I doubted anyone else paid close enough attention to his little ticks.

So admittedly, I had trouble staying glued to my phone, somewhat uninterested in the black-and-white of texting, but maybe I just needed more practice.

Neither of us could be classified as a typical teenager attached to a phone — sometimes I'd come back to my room midday only to realize I never took it off the overnight charger.

I looked through the available emojis, my recent ones were completely random, adding them sparingly to messages to Jess to make her laugh, and my phone vibrated, his response coming through almost immediately after I sent the text.

Texting you.

I begrudgingly chuckled, wondering how to interpret that. I needed more lines of text to read and overanalyze.

What else?

Looking at my phone.

I tried to picture him, in his pool house I've never set foot into, staring at his phone the same way I was.

And?

Waiting for Cor. He's working until 5.

My parents and Cory sat me down toward the end of the school year to announce that he would be taking on a full-time position at my parents' tax practice this summer, working forty hours a week doing something that I hadn't paid attention to at the time.

I bet Jeremy knew more about it than I did.

Cory had been to their office infinitely more times than I had, as a big advocate for "Take Our Kids to Work Day" every year, mostly because it got him a free pass from school.

But apparently, this year, something caught his eye, and he'd asked them if he'd be able to spend more time at the business, jumping at the chance when they offered him a real shot for minimum wage.

He came home excited each day, gushing about something he learned or experienced with a customer. I selfishly tuned him out, not caring that he seemed to actually be enjoying learning about the business and having a purpose to work toward.

I could see him working there long-term, maybe even taking over the business someday, in a perfect, easy future all mapped out for him.

The thought of that for myself gave me a stress headache, so I turned my thoughts back to Jeremy, my perfect, and very convenient, distraction.

Hang here with me while you wait?

The little flickering cloud with three dots, indicating

he was responding, started and stopped a few times before disappearing completely.

I watched it, waiting for it to reappear, and eventually gave up.

I hit the remote, and to my delight, "Speed" was still in the first act. Keanu just made the dive from the moving car onto the bus steps, and Sandra Bullock delivered her powerful line, setting the tone for the rest of the film: "This guy's out of his mind."

It flipped to a commercial, and I frowned, relegating myself to popcorn duty in the kitchen. I returned quickly, rearranging all of the pillows on my bed for prime movie-watching, and sank in, tossing a few kernels back.

One of the things I loved about action movies was the ability to get completely hooked into the story, with the comfort of knowing that everything was probably going to work out in the end.

Still, I couldn't help but yell at Helen as she went against Keanu's advice and tried to get off the bus, resulting in her immediate death. I sank back, frustrated.

"You have enough pillows there, Anna?"

I bolted upright from the pile of feathers and decorative tassels, knocking over the empty popcorn bowl, which Jeremy picked up and placed on top of my dresser. I'd been so lost in monitoring the bus' speedometer that I forgot he might be joining me.

I couldn't remember if I left the doors unlocked, practically an open invitation for some daytime mass murder to stroll right on in, only to recall that my parents did a big demonstration when the security system got installed for all of us — Cory, Jeremy, Jess, and I — on how to turn off the alarm before it beeped and notified the police.

"Seriously, your bed is covered with more pillows than I've ever seen someone have in one room," he said, diving on top of the bed next to me. "Oh, okay, I get it now."

He sunk in, using my favorite pillow to prop his head up, and I yanked it out from under him.

"This is my favorite," I explained, right as he opened his mouth. "You can use any of them but this one. It's mine."

He shook his head. "That only makes me want it more."

"Creepy," I said, locking my arms around it in a death grip.

He rolled his eyes. "Because it must be the best, not because I specifically can't have it."

His hands tugged at the fabric, and in fear of tearing it wide open, only to fill the air with one-thousand feathers, I gave up.

"Let's share it," I suggested, fluffing it up in a neutral spot between us.

I laid back, leaving a generous amount of room for him to lay next to me. He paused, weighing the situation, and I pretended to already be engrossed in the movie.

He slid down, extremely aware of our close proximity, and I breathed as normally as I could.

We watched the movie, getting more comfortable in each other's arms as he asked questions and we made fun of it, only slightly, during the commercial breaks.

In the end, as always, Keanu saved the day.

"What a romantic line," Jeremy scoffed. "'I didn't have anywhere to be just then.' That is what swooned her?"

"I always think about how ridiculous those situations for the actors must be, laying inside of an overturned subway car, making out as fake glass falls down from overhead. They probably had to do ten takes or something to get it just right, that perfect dismissiveness and smile, leading up to their big kiss."

"You know, that actually doesn't sound half bad."

"Acting?"

He shook his head. "Getting paid to kiss someone," he said, low and slow, turning toward me. "What's the cost for these?"

He ran his thumb along my bottom lip, and I panicked, biting down. Jeremy, however, thought it was cute, and playfully tickled my cheek with his pointer finger until I released him from the trap.

I swallowed. "A very high price," I said, my tone as serious as I could muster. "One worth sacrificing rules, all pretenses, and a little bit of dignity."

"Wow, that much, huh?"

"Or, I guess, another bowl of popcorn, maybe the Monster trail mix from Target, and oh, I think I have an unopened box of Trix in the pantry."

I mentally begged him to agree to the terms, as he pretended to really think it over, weighing the options thoroughly.

"You drive a hard bargain, but I accept."

He rolled over, the weight of his long body pinning me against the bed.

"What are you doing?" I gasped, wiggling underneath him.

"Collecting what I'm owed first," he said, pressing his lips against my neck and trailing upward. "I don't want you to back down. Or worse, charge me interest."

My normal, fidgety instinct would be to flee from some unexplainable embarrassment at our position, but when he leaned in, all the tension I held so tightly simply vanished. It was like Jeremy had this power over me to cause me to let go of everything, a reminder to do things just because I wanted to, and our kissing in the kitchen was my reaction to it. This, somehow, felt more deliberate.

His lips brushed mine, just barely, and we softened into each other.

I was opening up the endless possibilities that this summer could bring, and also, a little bit more to him.

My heart pounded in my ears as his mouth moved more urgently. I was acutely aware of everything, but at the same time, my mind was out of focus, and my body was in control. I dragged my leg against his, silently inviting him to touch more of me, and he did.

Without breaking apart, he slid his hand down my thigh, gripping it in a way that made me lose all the air in my lungs. I hooked it around his waist, catching the smirk against his lips before pressing him closer.

His hand slipped under my shirt, lazily tracing lines upward. It felt so good, natural to be like this with him, and I practically hummed under his touch.

Before I became completely lost in him, he pulled back. I registered the tortured look on his face, but I wasn't ready to end whatever this was. I tried pulling him down, but he held still, watching me.

"Totally worth it," he said, hopping up easily to make his way to the kitchen.

I brought my hand up to my mouth, needing to take many deep breaths to regain composure.

Just as I was reconciling this new version of myself, of him and me, my phone vibrated on the nightstand, sending me into another frazzled state.

"Jess, hey!" I answered, my voice a little higher than normal.

"Sorry I can't FaceTime because this cell service is shit here."

I leaned over to look at my reflection in the vanity mirror. My lips were swollen, my hair was a mess, and the rest of me was slightly disheveled. I'd never been happier for awful Florida coverage.

"It's okay," I said, swallowing. "I'm just happy to hear your voice."

"What are you doing? You sound weird. Did you try that meditation app I told you about?"

"No, sorry, I'm just, uh, watching a movie."

"Well I'm," she paused for dramatic effect, "gardening." She emphasized the word like it was shocking, a cruel and unusual punishment for her. "Did I tell you about how my grandmother thinks it is a fun activity for us to garden together? That's where I've been all day. All day! Baking in the sun and getting dirt in my nails. I'd been at it for forty-five minutes before she gave me gloves. I think part of her loves to see me all angry. Like it's entertaining or something."

"It does sound entertaining, honestly, I can't blame her after dealing with your high maintenance attitude," I admitted.

"Anna! I am not high maintenance, I am just who I am."

She continued rambling on as Jeremy stepped in, looking sheepishly handsome while carrying an armload of snacks, and I lost all sense of concentration.

"And that's why I decided against the pixie cut," she finished.

"Jess, I've got to go, 'Point Break' is starting," I said quickly. "Call you later."

I hit the end button and tossed my phone on the floor, which immediately started vibrating with texts from her. Ignoring it, I reached for the cereal box, wishing I was reaching for Jeremy instead, and tore it open.

"So you know how for a while, Trix have just been colorful round circles?"

"I don't, but continue," he said, feeding a handful of popcorn into his mouth.

"Well, they were like Kix, but General Mills just brought back the fruit shapes." I pulled open the plastic bag, picking out some of the lemon shapes to toss back. "I swear it makes them taste better."

"Fruit shapes, huh?"

He grabbed a handful, examining them closely, and I pointed to the little blue flower with a pink dot in the middle on his open palm. "This one is my favorite. They call it 'wildberry blue,' for some reason."

"That's not even a fruit."

"Valid point," I conceded. "I still love them."

"Are there even blue flowers in the world? Or do they just dye flowers blue and pink with artificial coloring?"

I scolded him. "Stop trying to ruin my Trix experience for me. I picked up this box specifically for nostalgia, not to have you be so judgmental."

Jeremy settled into the massive pile of pillows, feet dangling off the edge of the bed, as the second Keanu movie of the day began.

He remained unbothered as the garage door opened and closed, followed by heavy footsteps clunking up the two floors. I sat up in an unnatural position as Cory barged into the room, eyeing us suspiciously.

"What's going on?"

The accusation in his tone reverberated in my skull, and my blood pressure skyrocketed. I couldn't come up with one single thing to say.

"I came over here, looking for you," Jeremy said, as nonchalantly as only he could pull off. "Anna thought it'd be fun to induct me into her action movie cult."

He poured Trix straight from the box to his mouth, not spilling a single one, and I stared at him incredulously.

Cory sat down beside me, and I grabbed my pillow before he could get too comfortable on it.

"Oh, is this the one with Patrick Swayze?" His hand was already digging in on the container of trail mix. "Ha, and Gary Busey."

Jeremy nodded, eyes glued to the screen. "And the guy who played Dr. Cox on 'Scrubs.'"

"Don't you two have plans elsewhere?" I asked, watching Cory miss his mouth and get some of the coveted peanut butter chips on my white bedspread.

They both shrugged, and I tried my best to get lost in the film, finding difficulty with the two of them taking up so much space.

This wasn't my favorite movie. It didn't even really rank in the top twenty, but when Jeremy inconspicuously slid his hand into mine under the layers of pillows, I hoped it would never end.

7

SUMMER

BEFORE OUR BIG dance in eighth grade, Jess told me that in most cases it was better to be overdressed than under-dressed, and I didn't believe her.

I wore a short, simple pink dress with twisted straps and a jean jacket, and she was dressed immaculately, draped in a full ball gown, with gloves and everything, like a real-life Cinderella.

When we arrived at the event, we quickly discovered that I was, in fact, underdressed, and she was grossly the opposite. My moment of panic turned into laughter when she strode to the middle of the dance floor, showing that no one even broke out of their own vanity long enough to look at her.

"Who cares? Let's dance."

And we did.

I glanced at the picture from that night's photo booth, which was taped to my full-length mirror, and I, once again, wondered if I wasn't wearing the right clothes.

After spending weeks in cut-off shorts and skirts, that it felt strange to put on an actual dress. I didn't want to be seen as trying too hard or even trying at all, but Jeremy would know, and I felt strange about fretting over my appearance so much just to hang out with him.

I tightened the belt that matched the simple, dark blue shirt dress, and focused my attention to pulling out my curls, turning them to casual waves instead of perfect spirals.

"Anna, darling, come join us," my mother called from the bottom of the stairs. "We need to have a family meeting."

The formality of her tone made me nervous, and I wracked my brain for possible reasons for this that didn't have to do with me and the boy who was picking me up in ten minutes.

Last time we had a family meeting, it was to talk about Cory working for them, before that, my great aunt's death. Everything before it seemed like a blur.

The uncertainty of her request nipping at my thoughts was only heightened when I entered the kitchen. My parents and my brother sat at the table, all facing me like actors did on screen, which started to become really obvious to me once I started looking for it. My mom and dad seemed normal, in their after-work unwind stage of the day, but Cory had traded his basketball shorts and shirts with cut-off sleeves for a button-down and slacks.

"Why are you so dressed up?" I asked in the most uncomplimentary way, even though it was a good look for him.

"You know how Kathleen has been dodging me

asking her out?" He said it earnestly, like he'd already talked to me about this at length, so I nodded. "Well, it turns out she has a full-time administration internship at the hospital, and after that, she volunteers at the nursing home."

He seemed very proud, for someone who had absolutely nothing to do with her character development.

"Okay," I said, not connecting the dots that hadn't even been drawn yet.

"She wasn't just blowing me off, she was actually just busy," he explained, clearly excited. "So I signed up to volunteer on Tuesday nights, with her, and just this week she admitted she wanted to get to know me better. I'm taking her out and surprising her with a night downtown. She's been hinting about wanting to see some musical, and there's a good restaurant a few avenues away from it we're going to hit up before."

"Oh. That's nice." It actually was really nice — the first real gesture I'd ever known my brother to make for a girl. "So, is that it or can I go?"

I scooted sideways toward the door, hoping for a quick exit.

"Sit, Anna," my mother chirped, and I obliged her.

"So what's going on?" I asked, picking at my freshly painted nails.

My dad smiled. "We had some exciting news we wanted to talk to you about. With Cory finalizing where he is applying to college working out perfectly with him spending time at the business this summer, we think we have a plan."

"Plans are good," I offered, and they all nodded enthusiastically, like if three agreeable people had taken over the bodies of my family members.

"What your father is trying to say is that, well, Cory, do you want to tell her?"

"I'm going to apply to Duquesne and Drexel to double major in business and accounting," he explained, unable to suppress a giant grin. "That way I can take on more from Mom and Dad. Make a real impact and stuff."

"That's great news, Cory. But didn't we already have this conversation like three months ago?"

"Not necessarily in this context," my dad said. "We've also been in touch with Duquesne about creating some sort of for-credit program, where he can go to school and get on-site experience."

"So if Cory goes there, he can work on weekends, too, right? Lessen the overtime for you guys?"

More nods came from these alien people who were definitely not related to me.

"Cool," I said, feeling about eighty pounds of relief on what this conversation turned out to be.

I looked at the clock and realized I needed to meet Jeremy soon.

"Is that it?"

My mom reached out to hold my hand. "Well, sure, honey. But we just wanted to make sure you're okay with it."

"Why wouldn't I be?" I asked, more sharply than I intended.

"We've been putting a lot of thought into it and talking about the future. We're thinking that eventually, if Cory's still interested in it long-term, he can work to take over the business."

I tapped my foot, regretting not shooting Jeremy a text before I sat down. "Again, why wouldn't I be okay with this?"

"It's just that, well, we keep asking you what you want to do, and you always shut down."

"I don't shut down," I snapped. "I'm just sick of you guys always asking me about it. I've told you a billion times that I don't know."

My dad sighed. "And that's totally fine, Anna. You're young. You have time, but we're just trying to help you. Both of you. But if Cory takes on a bigger role, it could conflict with or lessen yours. If that's what you wanted to do."

I glanced at Cory, who crossed his arms. He looked mad, a one-eighty from when I joined this conversation. I was ruining this for him, I realized, accidentally making it all about me. His nostrils flared in irritation, and I took it as a signal to shut up and get out.

"That's fine with me," I said, checking my attitude. My parents eyed each other, and before they tried to re-explain to me their concern, I started again. "This seems like a win for the family. Thanks for checking with me, but I've got to go."

Three sets of eyeballs followed me as I walked out the front door.

Moments later, after cutting back up the path where Jeremy picked me up, I relayed the conversation to him, in part confusion.

"They just seemed so nervous telling me, like I was

going to stab them in the eyes with a kitchen knife or something."

He turned down the music from the buttons on the wheel. "Have you talked to them before about this?"

"About the business, no," I explained, flipping the air vent closed. "But about their incessant asking about my future, yes. It feels like pretty much every day. I'm tired of it."

"Why?"

I chewed on the inside of my cheek. "I just feel like everyone is trying to pressure me to make a decision, to pick my entire future. I don't have everything figured out, and more importantly, I don't want to."

"So instead, you don't want to make any decisions and that's how we're here because you realized that might have backfired since now you see everyone planning and experiencing and you have nothing?"

He wasn't wrong, but that didn't make it easier to hear. I bit my lip, forcing my stare out the window.

"You have to give people something, or they're going to give up on you, Anna."

He put his hand on my leg, slipping his fingertips under the fabric of my dress. "Jeremy!" I grabbed his hand to stop it from moving upward, and he laughed, successfully pulling me out of my contemplative spiral.

I slid my fingers between his.

"Just think about it, Anna."

"I will," I promised. "Thanks for listening."

He brought my hand up to his mouth, kissing the back on repeat, and I appreciated that he, too, put time in his appearance. I noticed his fresh shave when I jumped in the car, leaning over to kiss his cheek before launching into my story about my parents and Cory, but he also wore his best jeans, well worn and low on his waist, with a gray button-down.

The sight of him did strange but lovely things to my body.

"Prepare yourself, Anna. Tonight, we're branching out."

I gulped, realizing that I was in my own head, and he couldn't read my mind.

"More things off of the non-list list?" I asked, hopefully.

"I might have officially given up on that, but I had another idea."

"What?

"Other breakfast foods."

He pulled up to a diner, a semi-upscale one a few towns over, that attracted all sorts of people — those stopping through grabbing a cup of coffee all the way up to families of five out celebrating someone's birthday.

I tried to relax, staying light and out of my own head, but I was very aware of Jeremy's hand on my back as we stepped to the threshold. This suddenly felt very serious, date-like even, as the hostess led us past the dessert display case and toward a booth in the back.

I scanned the restaurant, nodding at the McKenzies, who lived a few houses up from mine, when we walked past.

We were seated, and I noticed a group of people from Jeremy's grade, and a few guys I recognized from the pool, in the far corner. Jeremy waved at his teammates, smiling, but the expression in his eyes was clear — do not come over here or bother us in any way.

Jeremy picked up the menu, scanning it slowly. "Do you think they have cereal?" He laughed at his own joke, flipping to see the featured entrees of the week.

"Jeremy, there are a lot of people we know here," I said, concerned. "Like a lot."

It would be too obvious, maybe even a little insulting, if I put our menus up on the table, like how our teachers used to make us do in grade school to stop people from cheating.

"So?" He said it in the least challenging way, like the thought had never, in one-million years, occurred to him that what we were doing would have any complications.

"What if they have questions? Or tell our parents we were out together?"

"I didn't realize it was a crime to be seen with me."

"Come on," I pleaded. "I'm kind of freaking out about it."

He put down his menu momentarily, patience wearing thin. "We'll just tell them we were waiting for Cory or avoiding the last-minute prep for tomorrow."

"Okay," I said, a little embarrassed.

He backtracked. "You've never really cared about fitting in with people, so there's no need to start now. Just think of it as part of the non-list list, channel my nonchalance about shit like this. People are going to talk, you can't control it, so why stress about it? Do you really think someone is going to stomp over here and demand answers?"

I glanced over my shoulder at Kim Patterson, who had

one of those names where you always had to say the first and last. She shot dangerous looks at me, eyeing me and whispering to the girl next to her, eyes scowling in my direction.

"I mean, Kim Patterson might. She looks like she's about to pounce on me, and I definitely feel like she would win in a fight against me, clawing out my eyeballs and laughing as I bled out."

Jeremy, to his credit, didn't even pay her any attention.

"Anna," he said, grasping my hand.

He circled his thumb around, and it instantly relaxed my mind. His eyes met mine, willing me to hear what he was saying carefully.

"Kim and I split up like six months ago. When she's not hyped up on coffee and Red Bull, which is practically never, she's funny and nice, but the more time we spent together, the more I realized she didn't have a lot going on in her mind other than texting me every fifteen minutes. In the end, it seemed like she wanted to be with me just to be with me for who I am to everyone else, not who I am as a person, so I broke it off. She got over it by sleeping with half the soccer team."

"Oh," I said, taken aback by his openness on a subject we'd never discussed. I cleared my throat. "So how do you think the pancakes are here?"

Jeremy chuckled. "Are you allergic to vegetables, Anna? I'm actually a little concerned at your vitamin intake. Maybe we should go to the pharmacy next."

"I had a salad for lunch," I admitted. Well, my plate had a salad on it. And I picked at it, after dousing it in ranch dressing. "But who comes to a diner and orders real food?"

"Me, in about three seconds."

The waitress came over to greet us and took our orders — grilled chicken for Jeremy and chocolate chip waffles for me. He gave me a "Really?" look after she left, and I laughed.

"Okay, Dad, I'll eat some of your broccoli."

"Don't call me that."

"Just because you're a sensitive, older man?"

"I'm less than a year older than you, Anna."

"How could I forget?" I said, flashing back to our shared memory bank. "You used to make me so angry when we were kids, hanging it over my head for no reason, really."

"No reason? I loved winding you up. I still do. Your nose gets all wrinkled, and you start to get all twitchy and fidgety."

"Hey now, you have some tells of your own, Jeremy."

"Like what?"

"Like how you tilt your head when you're really listening to me. And how you tap your thigh when you're excited. And when you don't want to talk about something, your left eyebrow moves down slightly while your teeth clench."

He put his elbows on the table, adjusting his stance, and I realized I went too far. His demeanor changed from light banter to a serious, challenging tone. "Ask me anything," he baited. "I'm an open book."

I took a long sip of water. "You don't want to play basketball," I told him. "I could tell when I brought it up in the kitchen, and since then, I've noticed you go through the motions just to please your dad when your heart isn't into it. I'm right, aren't I?"

He twirled the empty straw wrapper. "I haven't told anyone this. Not even Cory." He scratched his jaw and took a deep breath. I readied myself for a deep confession, but all I got was one sentence. "I'm a mediocre basketball player."

I scoffed. "Now that's absolutely not true. No way, Jeremy, I've seen you play so many times, and playing at a level or two ahead of everyone else."

"You don't believe me, but I promise it is the truth. I'm the best out of who I'm playing now, but when I get to college, I'm going to get destroyed. I seem tall to you, but can you imagine me playing against guys who are six-six? I wasn't kidding when I mentioned that my dad is counting on a growth spurt."

"I never thought about it like that," I admitted, realizing what a relief it must be for him to get this out of his own head. "So where do you want to go? What do you want to do?"

"I was thinking Pitt, just not for basketball, or maybe, you know how they have those college events at school every spring? I talked to the woman at Point Park for a while. They have an awesome journalism program, and I'd be interested in doing sports broadcasting or something like that. Still involved but not necessarily sweating it out on the court."

I imagined Jeremy, a future, older version of him chopping it up with a bunch of celebrity athletes and being

Twitter famous. "I can see it. I really can. With your personality, it makes sense."

He licked his top lip. "And my good looks."

"And your modesty, clearly."

He ran a hand through his hair, smile fading quickly. "I just haven't figured out a way to tell my dad."

"I don't think it will be as bad as you think."

"Have you met Mark Blake?"

"Oh come on, after three martinis at my dad's poker night last month, I overheard him get a little weepy with pride over you. It would definitely be tough for him at first, to give up his dream of having a son for an athlete, but he has to realize that's not your dream."

He processed my words, staring at the pattern on the table.

"Of course, you know your mom will back you up," I nudged him lightly. "And if all else fails, my parents, hell, anyone in my family who has met you and already likes you more than me, would take you in."

He stared at me for a few beats, and I grew self-conscious. "What?" I asked.

"I'm just," he paused, giving a slow, sexy smile, "really glad to be with you."

I flushed, and our food arrived. We dug into our dinner, and although we picked on each other for our ordering preferences, we ended up pushing both plates in the middle and splitting everything. We argued about how all eggless breakfast food is essentially dessert. We psychoanalyzed all of Cory's past girlfriends. We laughed at embarrassing moments growing up. He quizzed me about my past romantic experiences. And most importantly, we tuned out everyone else around us.

I placed my napkin on the table, calling it quits, and headed to the bathroom.

As I was touching up my mascara in the mirror, the door swung open. I braced myself, in fear that Kim Patterson and her rage followed me, but a tall, red-haired Rhea McKenzie stepped in.

"Oh, hey Rhea."

"Hi Anna," she said, all business, as she walked right up to me.

I stepped sideways, glancing at our reflections in the mirror. "How's your summer going?" I asked. "I heard you're working on some really cool art project."

"Is there anything going on between you and Jeremy?"

She blinked, and I almost stabbed myself blind with the wand.

"What do you mean?" I asked, putting it back in the holder. Of course, I missed and spread inky black goop all over my fingers. I hurried to wash it off.

She flipped her hair over her shoulder.

"Well, you're here with him on a Friday night and seem pretty cozy," she said, explaining it as if I was a pesky three-year-old. "To be honest, I've been trying to work up the nerve to talk to him forever, and if you're not together, I was going to walk over to ask him out right now."

"Oh, uh, we're not together," I mumbled. "We're just waiting on Cory. Avoiding our parents and the setup for the fundraiser and all that. Really, just casually eating. Like normal people who know each other and are neighbors and watch movies and stuff like that, you know."

She ignored my awkwardness. "Great!" She clapped and walked right back out.

"Great!" I said, mocking her tone, to my mirrored reflection.

I brought my hands up to my face, wondering how the hell I became a jealous green monster after that conversation. I stalled in the bathroom and then stomped out, just in time to see a smiling Rhea heading back to the table with her family.

Jeremy, however, looked furious when I slid back in across from him.

"You told her nothing is going on with us?"

"Did I do that?" I curled a piece of hair around my fingertips. "I'm not sure those are exactly the words I used when she accosted me in the bathroom."

"Well, then let me choose my exact words very carefully here, Anna." He leaned in, straightening up to deliver the message. "I definitely think there is something going on."

It sat between us, that truth he just told, right there on the table. I fought it with everything I had, unwilling to accept it.

"Is that what you told her?" I barely hid the bite to my tone. "Because that's a lie."

"How?" he asked, his voice low but sharp.

I wracked my brain for some explanation that could keep us suspended from reality for a little longer. "Where I sit, there's nothing. A whole lot of nothing. I want to do things this summer, go places, get in trouble. A lot of things off of my non-list list, and so far, I've done nothing, and you're supposed to be helping me!"

It was new for me, to become a possessive, selfish version of myself, but I didn't mind it. Instead of one very boring person, I felt like one-thousand people all at once, overflowing with emotion and desire.

Jeremy watched me squirm in my explanation but offered nothing in return.

I didn't really mean what I said, but he agreed to spend time with me, and he was going to have to deal with my new rough emotions.

He edged closer to me, knocking our knees together under the table.

"What do you really want, Anna? What's this all about?"

My gaze dropped to my hands, twisting and shaking in my lap. I knew if I spoke right away my voice would be thick with emotions, the kind that always surface when people ask if you're okay and you're not but you lie.

Talking was exhausting. I was tired of being in my own head, absorbing every word and scrutinizing the true intention. I closed my eyes briefly, recalling the last two times I'd truly felt weightless, and I knew what I wanted — hell, what I needed more than anything at that moment.

Ignoring all rationale, I exhaled. "I want to feel things, Jeremy," I said, my voice lowering to a whisper. "I want to feel you."

I expected him to be unhinged by my confession, some sort of sultry revelation breaking him down into a puddle at my feet, but if anything, he seemed skeptical.

"Anna, what's with you? An hour ago you didn't want

to be seen with me, and now you're practically begging me to take your clothes off in the middle of this restaurant."

I could be that girl in the kitchen again, forward and fearless, and I moved my hands under the table, sliding them up his legs, oh-so-slowly.

"Is that what it takes, Jeremy?" I asked, quietly. "Do you want me to beg for you?"

He swallowed, a sign of his resolve wavering. "Check please," Jeremy called out to our approaching waitress.

8

SUMMER

It was the longest thirty-minute drive of my life.

I couldn't keep my hands off of him, caressing every part I could reach, pulling the seat belt tight across my chest. His breath moved rapidly, his eyes flickering between me, the road, and the speedometer.

Each time we hit a red light, his mouth was on mine, hard and fast, only to be ripped apart again by the sound of a honking horn behind us when the light turned green.

He gripped my thigh, turning sharply into his driveway. I cringed when the tires squealed slightly, but he stopped short, leaving his car far from the exposure of the floodlight.

He threw the gear in park, turned off the ignition, and swung around to open my door for me before my shaking hands even managed to undo my seat belt.

I threw myself at him, hitting against the fence, and his hands slid up my back. He pushed us toward the back gate, and after nearly tripping several times as I tried to keep him pressed up against me, he took control.

We slipped through the small gap in the tall hedges, his strong grasp on my wrist leading me through, and the thought occurred to me that I might not have been the first one he'd snuck in this way, which made me more nervous than anything else.

I tripped over one of the small pieces of shrubbery, and he caught me and stepped up, bringing me to his chest. I inhaled as he slid his hands from my waist to my thighs, then my ass, and pulled me up into his arms. I caught his ear with my tongue, and his arms tightened on my skin.

Jeremy walked like he kissed, with unfathomable confidence and urgency, but I'd never seen him move so quickly. His eyes blazed ahead with purpose, like none I'd ever seen before.

In all the years watching him on the court or solving a complex homework problem on our kitchen table, I never imagined I'd see him like this, so determined to be with me.

After fumbling with the keys at the door, he dropped me, gently. I already felt empty out of his arms, and I ignored how terrified that made me feel. We stepped inside, and he locked the door behind us then pulled the blinds down, and stood motionless in the window, making sure we were in the clear.

I kicked off my sandals and started to undo the knot of my dress, and he froze, the air in the room nearly sucked out as he watched me, fists clenched at his side. I held his gaze as I undid the buttons, one at a time, and dropped the fabric at my feet, kicking it aside.

His mouth was at mine in an instant. I met his desperation, arching my back as his tongue parted my lips, deepening the kiss. My hands moved on their own volition, sliding up to trace the lines of his muscles. Jeremy paused momentarily, grabbing the hem of his shirt and lifting it overhead.

A smile dangled at the corner of his mouth as we moved to the bed, a monstrosity in the middle of the room. The back of my knees caught against the frame, and I sat down, peering up at him. He slid off his shoes, gaze dipping down over my exposed skin, expelling a breath as his hands moved to his belt.

"Let me do it," I demanded, in a voice that was so raspy I wasn't completely certain it was my own.

Somewhat clumsily, I undid the buckle and button. My hands shook as I slid the zipper, and then the denim, down. His hands gripped my hair to hold my head in place, as his teeth tugged at my bottom lip. I closed my eyes, and his fingers flicked, unclasping my bra.

He pulled back, watching me as we crossed this unspoken barrier. I flipped my hair behind me, giving him a full view of my exposed chest, and suddenly, his tongue was there, and I was breathless. I pushed into him, digging my nails into his back as he swirled around. I could barely suppress the moan.

"Anna," he breathed. "Anna, I..." He trailed off, sitting beside me with a thud.

I opened my eyes to see his pupils dilated, his body practically shaking with need, but his brow was pulled into a crease. I shifted my leg over his to straddle him, and his hands were at my hips in an instant.

"Be here with me, Jeremy."

He shook his head, but his grip tightened against the thin fabric at my waist. "I am," he said, quietly. "I'm just, I don't know, caught up in all of this."

I ignored him, begging him with my body for more. I moved my hips down, grinding against him, and he groaned. But he didn't give in.

"You've had no problem with casual sex in the past," I reminded him.

"Correct," he admitted, rubbing his hands where the lace met my upper thigh.

I touched his chest, confirming his heart was about to pound straight through his skin.

"So what's the issue?" I asked, snaking my arms back up to lock behind his head.

"This isn't casual sex."

"Yes, it is."

A wary smile overtook his lips. "It isn't casual for me, Anna."

I shook my head, mentally pleading with him to not say anything else. He pulled me closer. "It isn't," he insisted.

I sighed, settling into the blissfulness of him touching my skin.

"Tell me there's something here."

Our lips met, and with every swipe of my tongue, every rock of my hips, every second that passed, I tried to coax him back.

"Anna, come on," he pleaded, holding me in place. "This isn't nothing. We're doing something, and I need to hear you say it."

I traced his jawline, pausing for a second to acknowledge that his needs weren't just physical, ignoring the pang of realization that mine likely weren't either. "This isn't nothing, Jeremy."

He shifted his hips and rolled over, pressing every inch against me. I practically convulsed as he moved his hand slowly, tracing the line of my body, slipping a finger under the only fabric that remained. I arched up, and his head moved down to my chest, once again, and I almost came undone from a swipe of his tongue.

"Am I your first?"

The question, asked so softly, hung in the air, but he didn't stop touching me, in a way that made the others I'd been with seem so foolish, completely beneath his league that it was laughable. I nodded against his mouth, and suddenly, an overwhelming nervousness wracked my body.

He inhaled sharply, and he pulled back, supporting his weight on his elbows and knees.

Being with him was like nothing I'd ever experienced before, like every inch of me was electrically charged for this exact moment. I loved feeling so exposed under his gaze, and I wanted this, so much. Parts of me ached for it, actually, and I'd fantasized about it endlessly, so I couldn't comprehend why my own body was betraying me at this moment in his bed.

Outright panic stirred inside me, threatening to ruin what was pretty much guaranteed to be the best night of my entire life.

He kissed me, lightly. "You're not ready."

"Don't tell me that I'm not ready," I said, bitterly, letting my vulnerability stir up defensiveness. "You don't know that."

He bit his lip, choosing his words. "You're not ready to let go of everything and just feel. That's what you wanted, wasn't it? The goal of all of this?"

I surrendered into the mattress, letting my arms fall above me. "I need to think, Jeremy," I explained to the ceiling. "It's how the human brain works."

"Anna, you're shaking."

"I'm nervous as hell, but I want this," I promised. "I want you more than I've wanted anything in my entire life."

"More than that Barbie dream car you didn't get for your seventh birthday?"

I smiled. "Yes. Infinitely. If infinity times infinity existed, it might come close to how much more."

He tucked my hair behind my ears, registering what I'd said, and I swallowed, wondering how the hell he could recall such a thing. I would worry about that later, I decided, and fell into the bliss of ignorance. I dragged my fingertips along the top line of his boxer briefs, making him shudder.

His body jerked, and his hand slipped behind my neck, pulling me up to crush his lips against mine. His thumb hooked at my waistband, sliding my remaining shred of modesty down, and I returned the favor. I glanced down, reeling in the incredible feeling of being completely bared to him.

With our bodies so damn close, I felt on fire, desirable even, but it wasn't enough. I was throbbing from our extended foreplay, and I needed to work toward my release, but he beat me to it, building me up. He rubbed in circles, and I gripped the sheet, almost completely coming apart when he slid a finger, and then two, inside me.

"Let go," Jeremy whispered, moving his hand faster.

And I did, while gripping his hair and calling his name in the darkness. I caught his tongue with mine, feeding into the frenzy of hormones and pleasure of emotion radiating through my body. He planted dozens of kisses as I came down from the high.

He lazily moved his hand up my arm. "Remember when you asked me if I thought you were hot?"

I nodded, from somewhere far above, maybe in the clouds.

"You're hot. Unbelievably so. But seeing that was a new level, enough to drive me insane. The hottest thing I've ever seen and then some."

I laughed at his honesty, catching his mouth in mine. He deepened our kiss, and I moved my hand downward, hoping he'd guide me to him. Instead, he leaned over, pulling open the drawer next to the bed, and my heart thumped in my ears.

"It's going to hurt," he warned, tearing open a packet. "But I want it to feel good for you, Anna. Tell me if it doesn't feel good."

"I will," I promised, watching him roll the condom on.

I swallowed, and he smirked, pushing my legs open.

His entire body flexed as he moved inside me, the most unbelievable sight of us coming together. His hips rolled, and my toes curled in the mix of pleasure and pain.

"Anna, you feel," he lost the words, moving tediously, inch by inch, inside me.

I couldn't stop the tears from welling up. Every part of me buzzed, every sense heightened, and it was intoxicating. His eyes met mine, wincing at my discomfort.

"Do you want me to stop?"

I shook my head, and he trailed kisses along my jaw.

He slid his arms behind my back, holding onto my shoulders, and with his hooded eyes locked on mine, he pushed through. I gasped, gripping his waist. One-thousand thoughts flew through my head, and at the same time, nothing existed except for him and me.

We fed off of each other's moans and movement, and gave in, completely. I met him, riding upward until he found his release and collapsed beside me. He held me close, both of us panting and sweating, limbs tangled.

"Anna," he breathed, checking to make sure I was all right.

I kissed him once more, assuring him, and we talked, lightly, until his steady breaths led him into unconsciousness.

I slipped out, letting myself into the small bathroom to clean up.

For the second time tonight, I stared at myself in the mirror, contemplating every single thing. I had the same boring brown eyes I always had, same long semi-wavy hair, same everything else. But I felt different, like I'd tapped into a part of myself that needed to be discovered.

I traced my fingers over my mouth, my lips a little swollen, and couldn't help but grin.

9

SUMMER

I NEVER REALLY APPRECIATED OR understood the purpose of centerpieces, but my mother insisted they were a crucial component of every gathering.

Yet every holiday and event she hosted, her quest to find the perfect assortment of sparkle, flowers, and ribbons for the table seemed to be a distraction, a place to bucket much of her stress and worry in her role as hostess.

Last Thanksgiving, for example, she fretted about what to get for weeks, taking regular trips to the crafts stores around town and scouring online for inspiration. She even made me create a Pinterest account for her, and I have to admit I was pretty proud of the organization of it all. Eventually, she came home with some giant vase, ready to be filled with cranberries, taking the time to glue leaves on the side, which cascaded over the table cloth. She showed it off to every single guest who came through the door, and once we sat down, with plates full of turkey and mashed potatoes, we all had to crane our necks if we wanted a chance at hearing the other side of the conversation.

As a privately funded venture, I chalked it up to a nice hobby for her, but I was slightly terrified to step under the tent at the fundraiser to see at least fifteen unfinished centerpieces.

"Oh good, Anna, you're here," my mother said, handing over a bag of red, white, and blue pinwheels. "Help me do the rest like that one."

She gestured to a triple-tiered setup of American flags, red flowers, blue glittery stars, and what appeared to be every single other Fourth of July–themed decoration from the craft store. Ostentatious, a word I relearned in my SAT prep, described it perfectly.

I inwardly groaned but sat down beside her to help, settling into the small talk as other volunteers joined the table, catching up on the latest gossip.

Occasionally, someone would come up to my mom to ask her a question, and without breaking her stride, she directed them to the correct spot or contact, or she'd casually pick up her phone, roping someone else in to help out.

It was actually kind of nice, I realized, to be included in the process, and even better to see my mom put her planning and supervising skills to something other than me.

"Mom, question," I said, dropping my voice so only the two of us could hear. "Does it seem kind of weird to spend all of this money on a party, when we could just donate it to the shelter?"

She glanced around, eyeing the caterers setting up the carving station and heat lamps.

"Tax deductions, my dear," she beamed, and the whole thing seemed kind of gross to me. Catching my expression, she added, "I'm kidding, Anna. Did you know even moms can be funny?"

I laughed reluctantly.

"If we just asked people to give money, like we've done so many times, very few would actually participate," she answered, more seriously. "But when we started hosting these fundraising events a few years ago, donations went up by more than two-thousand percent."

"Two-thousand?" I nearly shrieked.

She nodded. "Believe it or not, Anna, people like feeling like they're a part of something. So many businesses around the area jumped at the chance to help, donating things like massages and weekend getaways, which we'll, in turn, raffle off for triple what they're worth. And, for the third year in a row, Mark Blake Dentistry is matching all donations."

"He likes to hold the giant check," Alicia said, sitting down next to me.

She fanned her face with her hand, and I smiled.

"Sharon, these are coming along great."

My mom sat back, admiring her handiwork. "I think so."

"The boys are finishing setting up all the tables and chairs now."

I turned my head over my shoulder to see Jeremy and Cory pull chairs off of a cart, slipping red covers on top of them.

Jeremy laughed at something Cory said, and I couldn't help but smile. Seeing him enjoying himself made me happy, too, even in the middle of Uncle Sam and Rosie the Riveter's reincarnation celebration.

My chin hit my palm, and I waited to catch Jeremy's eye.

How long had he been here? What was I doing when he first saw me? Did his heart leap like mine just did?

My mom put her hand on my arm to get my attention. "Anna, are you listening?"

"Start placing the centerpieces on the tables?" I guessed correctly, and she nodded, giving me very specific orders on how to make it perfect.

I grunted under the weight, dragging one of the creations over to Cory and Jeremy. I dropped it, with a clang, and checked to make sure that nothing broke. Jeremy's hands appeared, sliding the display to the center of the table while I held the cloth in place.

"Hi," I said, a little sheepishness crept up when Jeremy finally turned to face me.

He gave me his slyest smile. "Hi."

"How are you?"

"Good," he answered. "And you?"

I bit my lip. "Good."

"Good or really good?"

"Great," I laughed.

"Me too."

Cory knocked two of the chairs together. "You two are weirding me out. I'm going to take the cart back, Jeremy, then your mom wants us to help pack up the boxes before people arrive."

He patted the table, a sign of finality, and mumbled to himself as he walked away.

Jeremy leaned a little closer. "I brought you something."

"A gift?" I asked. "This isn't a gift-giving holiday. I didn't get you anything."

He dropped his chin. "You gave me the ultimate gift last night."

He walked me over to a pile of blankets and bags. Rifling through them, he pulled out a small bunch of blue flowers wrapped in plastic.

"They're not the same as the Trix flowers, but at least the color's right."

I brought them up to my nose, inhaling the summery, light scent. "I love them! Thank you."

I resisted the urge to step up and kiss him, but I couldn't suppress the grin, nearly choking on the thoughtfulness of his gesture. I extended my arm, and he brought me to his chest.

"Almost as beautiful as you, Anna," he whispered. For a second, we held each other, just like we did through the early hours of the morning.

"Anna?" Mrs. Lewis, Jess's mom, said, breaking our embrace to pull me in for a hug of her own. "Oh, Anna, it's been ages."

Jeremy's eyebrows raised as Mrs. Lewis rocked me back and forth, pure happiness radiating from her expression. Normally I'd wiggle out of it, uncomfortable with the attention, but her overwhelming presence added to my exuberance of the past twenty-four hours. Jess and her mom had the biggest personalities of any room, and it was like I had a piece of her there with me.

"Mrs. Lewis, have you met Jeremy Blake?" I asked,

fumbling on how exactly to introduce him. "We're neighbors."

"It's nice to meet you," he said, politely and sincerely, extending his hand.

She shook it, eyeing him up. "You're the egotistical basketball player who is the best friend of boneheaded Cory, correct?" She dropped his hand and laughed at his surprise. "I'm just going off of the descriptions my Jessica uses. Don't take offense."

"None taken," he assured her but looked at me sideways, eyes pleading for help. "How is Jess doing this summer? Enjoying her trip?"

"I'm sure Anna knows better than I do. I stopped answering her calls. Can't listen to her complain anymore about her all-expenses-paid summer vacation to Florida. Must be so hard!"

"Aww, Mrs. Lewis, she just misses you so dearly," I joked.

She tilted her head to look at me over her gigantic sunglasses. "Now we both know that isn't true." She readjusted her bag on her shoulders. "If you'll point me in the direction of your mother, I'll get out of your hair. I have some illegally purchased goods to light up this evening."

"Would it even really be the Fourth of July without them?" I asked, good-naturedly. "Annual traditions and all that."

"Anna doesn't even like fireworks," Jeremy jumped in, and my jaw dropped open at his betrayal. "She thinks, her words not mine, that they are 'juvenile.' I just thought it was my responsibility to clarify that for you, as your new favorite egotistical basketball player."

Mrs. Lewis cracked a toothy smile. "Oh, I like you."

"My mom is over by the caterers, straight back there," I said in a flat tone.

"Don't sulk, Anna, it makes you age prematurely," she called, making her way across the grass. "And tell my Jessica to stop it, too!"

I turned to Jeremy, mock anger crossing my features. "We're fighting now."

"Oh, come on, Anna. Don't get jealous because other women think I'm charming."

"What is it with you and Jess both being interested in older married people?" I asked, smoothing down my dress.

"What?"

I inhaled, realizing who I was telling this to. "You both are infectiously flirty around adults."

"Given the choice, I'd rather flirt with you."

He stepped forward, and I put my hand on his chest. "I can practically feel my mom scolding me for neglecting my centerpiece duties."

Jeremy set off to join Cory, and I caught up to Mrs. Lewis and stuck by her side for the next few minutes, until my mom and Alicia directed me to roll silverware, tying it up with a bow.

It seemed like an insult to put the blue flowers in my purse, so I wrapped them up in a cloth napkin, zipping them out of the back pocket carefully, and hoped they wouldn't get smashed.

The next two hours passed by in a whirl of directing volunteers, arranging the silent auction, and ensuring the cotton candy machine found the proper generator. The day cooled off, falling into a warm, lovely evening as more people arrived to help.

By the time the event started, more than ten-thousand dollars had been raised for the local shelter, not including the promised bids for the silent auction and raffles.

Under the dark sky, I could finally relax. I pulled myself out of the umpteenth conversation with adults, and the inevitable "What are your plans after high school?" question, for a moment of solitude on the sidelines. The event was on a huge, flat, grassy area just below massive, tree-covered hills.

When we were kids, we found a perfect sled-riding path between some of the trunks, using it almost religiously every snow day until Cory flew off his toboggan and broke his arm.

Now, with the twinkle lights, music, and laughter, I felt decades older mentally, even allowing a sense of pride in my part in helping create this setting.

As if he could sense my unguarded state, Jeremy snuck up behind me. "Can I take you somewhere?"

I nodded, and with his hand in mine, we slipped away.

He led me up to the path, through the trees. We moved silently, the only sounds were our footsteps breaking fallen branches and the diminishing chatter from the people below. Above us, the sky turned from a grayish blue into the deeper black of night, and we finally reached the top.

He pulled me to him, our chests moving rapidly together. And in the most romantic and utterly cliché moment of my life, he kissed me as the fireworks began.

We sank to the ground, grappling for each other, to

watch the show. This was the best view I could have imagined — purples, reds, and blues bursting above us, and Jeremy, right there with me.

When the sky finally darkened and smoky hues remained, I sighed, finding the comfort of silence and his embrace.

"Care to change your stance on this holiday?"

I shook my head. "But this, by far, is the best one I've ever had."

"Agreed. Mrs. Hannover really crushed it with the desserts this year."

My arm hit his in annoyance. He laughed, but I could barely see his smile.

"It's getting late," I said, begrudgingly.

He extended a hand to help me up, and it took us a lot longer to get to the bottom than it did to the top, deterred by the combination of stopping for make-out sessions and fumbling around in the pitch black.

When we slipped back into the crowd, something tugged at me instantly, and I turned to Jeremy, his eyebrows pulled in with the same suspicions as me.

I held onto him, and he politely pushed us through the circle of people, stopping suddenly enough for me to bounce off of him and into Cory.

Mark stood in the middle of the event, slurring and yelling at his shell-shocked wife, with my parents both timidly stepping around him with their arms up, trying to reason with him.

He yelled somewhat incoherently, as Alicia graciously tried to persuade him to leave. I put my hand on Jeremy's waist, causing Cory to snap his gaze to us, narrowing at our stance.

"Jeremy, I think you're going to have to intervene," I said quietly, eyeing the expressions of the remaining party guests.

He nodded, a mixture of pity and anger evident on his features, and stepped forward with Cory following close behind him.

"Hey Dad," Jeremy called, approaching cautiously.

Mark stood up straight, swaying slightly, and reached out, pulling Jeremy into him. "My boy! My star! Where have you been? I've been looking for you."

Cory glanced at me, and I kept my gaze straight ahead.

"I wanted to introduce you to someone." Mark glanced around, the glassiness reflecting off of his eyes.

"Actually, Dad, do you mind taking me home?" Jeremy asked him. "I have early practice planned for tomorrow."

He sputtered momentarily, taking an uneasy step forward. "Of course. Of course. Of course."

"I'll drive," Alicia said firmly, leading the charge over to their car.

Cory and Jeremy delicately guided him to the back seat, where he promptly collapsed. My parents jumped into crisis dissolution mode, thanking everyone for coming and for their donations. The four of us stayed behind in silence, making sure that the clean-up was in order before we piled into my dad's car.

I watched the oversized, fake check get tossed into the dumpster as we drove off.

It was sad how many times we'd seen Mark act like that, but it had gotten worse in the past few years, and I wondered what attributed to it. They had a happy life, a comfortable one, but there seemed to be a hole that only booze could fill.

My heart ached for the embarrassment Jeremy and his mom likely felt at something that was totally out of their control.

I took a long shower, holding onto that feeling of him while needing to rinse off the end of the night. My thoughts filled with Jeremy, how light and happy we were moments before, and I wish we'd stayed up on that hill instead.

My phone buzzed as I pulled on my favorite pair of sleep shorts and a long shirt.

Can I interest you in another sleepover?

I laughed, glancing at the blue flowers that were on my nightstand in a glass of water.

You mean the kind where we braid each other's hair and paint our nails and gossip about all the cute boys at school?

No... the kind where we are both naked and moaning each other's names.

I held my phone to my chest, my body already ready for more.

I'll be at the pool house in 10.

10

FALL

A MONTH AGO, I stormed into Jeremy's pool house, after spending the rest of the day reeling from his disruption in class.

I spewed obscenities, chided him for embarrassing me on purpose, and demanded an explanation for why he was acting like such an asshole. I wanted to verbally smack the look of overconfidence off of his face, but by the end of my spiel, I was warm and red-faced, and he was at an all-time high of smugness.

"Stop it," I seethed.

"Stop what? Stop remaining quiet while you get all of your feelings out? Stop being patient while you put all of these ridiculous reasons in your head of why we're not together? Stop sitting here listening to you tear apart my personality?" He threw his arms up. "Stop what exactly?"

My jaw tightened.

"Just stop, Jeremy," I pleaded. "I don't want the attention." I put my hands on my hips, squaring up against him.

"No, let me clarify, I don't want your attention. The summer is over. We're over, and I'm asking you to follow through with that."

A mix of sadness and helplessness passed over his features for a few seconds, and I swallowed the burning tightness in my throat.

He sat back, stretching his arms over his head, taking long, deep breaths.

"Just get out, Anna."

The dryness in his request held my feet in place.

My brain, at that exact moment, seemed to register where I was standing, the room where Jeremy and I opened up to each other, completely. I'd been so vulnerable then, for other reasons, and I didn't know how I stood here, weeks later, in a similar yet totally different state.

"Jeremy, how did we let—"

"I'll leave you alone," Jeremy promised, turning his back. "But you need to leave me first."

His muscles were locked in anticipation for my reaction, and my betraying fingers wanted to run along them. I squeezed my eyes shut, giving the tears permission to roam down my cheeks, and I left.

My hands shook as I put the keys in the ignition, drove straight to Jess's house, and collapsed into her open arms.

I told her everything, and for the most part, she was silent, taking it all in. Her expressions varied as I told her about the first night when we made a pact, the tattoo parlor, the gestures that made me melt, the pool house, and everything else.

By the end, her kitchen countertop was almost completely covered in tissues, and the sticky ice cream carton she pulled out from the freezer mid-way through my confession was now completely empty — just like me.

We sat there in silence for a minute, and she piled her hair up on the top of her head, securing it with an elastic.

She wrung her hands together in frustration, and I braced myself for the wrath she was about to unleash on Jeremy and my memory of him.

"You're an idiot, Anna."

My mouth dropped open. "What?" I snapped, one-hundred percent baffled.

"And I can't believe you didn't tell me when this was all happening."

"I don't think I knew how," I admitted.

"I just can't believe I never saw this coming. I mean, it's kind of perfect, if you think about it. The two of you. I always thought he had a thing for you." She eyed my look of surprise. "Oh come on, Anna. Think of how he always looked at you. How he treated you when we were kids? And who he spent his time with? Kim Patterson? That Lacy girl before that? A bunch of other blondes with absolutely no chance at something long-term? It's like he was waiting around for you to wake up."

I dropped my head on the counter, totally spent emotionally.

"I still can't believe Jeremy had a boner for your weird eating habits and actually suffered through those movies with you. Frankly, the patience of a saint that one has, taking you on like the most perfect dates ever. New respect for him, even after I had to listen to my mom gush about how handsome he is for weeks after you introduced them."

Jess threw her arms around my back, tilting her head against mine.

"Anna, I have to be honest with you," she said, squeezing me tighter. "When the time comes where you're ready to confront the reality of your feelings for him and what that means, I really hope he is still ready to be with you. Because someday, and I hope it's soon, you're going to regret being such a top-notch bitch to him."

"You're supposed to be my best friend," I accused, as my voice broke. "You're supposed to be on my side."

"Oh, I am," she said, reluctantly. "Of course I am. Jeremy can act like an overgrown baby sometimes trying to get attention, but you're reacting out of fear. You use your inability to get tied down as a badge of honor, and I think we're getting to the point where you're going to have to stop being so paralyzed. People have mental blocks about commitment. It's not me, but I get it on some level. Still, you're going to have to make decisions, some of them right, a lot of them wrong."

I chewed on my bottom lip, letting her words sink in.

"But you're going to have to do something. It's normal to be scared, but you're terrified. And honestly, tough love moment, you have no reason to be. It's not like you have some tragic backstory or suffered through your parents' ugly divorce."

For the first time, I felt guilty. I'd been acting like a spoiled, insensitive brat at the cost of other people's feelings. I started to apologize, but Jess cut me off.

"Anna, I know that action movies are your preferred source of entertainment, but even those movies have themes just like this one. Like, I don't know, didn't Indiana

Jones have commitment issues with that one woman who was perfect for him, and they had Shia LaBeouf? And then there were aliens?"

I rubbed my eyes. "Not exactly, but I guess I understand the point you're trying to make."

"What about the 'Terminator' movies or 'Rocky' or something?"

Despite it all, I smiled. "Now you're just reciting movies I've tried to make you watch."

She threw our spoons in the dishwasher, and I helped her clean up the rest of the mess we made.

"If it makes you feel better, I promise to watch one of those movies with you this weekend."

"You'd sit through the original 'Terminator' with me? Actually, no, the second one is the best. Oh, I should make you watch 'Die Hard' instead, but wait, no it's too early for a Christmas movie."

"I regret this already," she admitted, pulling me into a hug.

Her support was unwavering as I clenched my fists every time I passed Jeremy in the hall or had a momentary relapse of sadness because of him. True to his word, he left me alone, but occasionally I'd turn to grab something from my backpack at lunch or look up in a classroom and catch his eyes before I quickly diverted my own.

I almost didn't recognize him the day he strolled into the cafeteria with his hair buzzed.

Jess followed my eye line. "Oh shit," she breathed in. "I forgot how he pulls off that whole 'escaped convict' look so well."

I glared at her, even though I was thinking the exact same thing.

My fingers remembered the feeling of his curls twisted up, and I wondered what it would feel like to run my hand over his head right now. It was getting chilly outside, enough where he'd need a hat to stay warm, and I spent the rest of lunch and most of both Chemistry periods imagining how sexy he'd look in one of those slouchy winter hats.

"Uh oh," Tim groaned, and the mixture in front of us started to bubble over.

I grabbed paper towels, trying to stop the mess from spreading, but my efforts became futile when the beaker cracked, spraying a non-toxic but foul-smelling liquid all over my shirt.

Mrs. Blake sent me off to the bathroom to try and clean up, and I pulled at the fabric, hoping the scent wouldn't linger on my skin.

I rounded a corner and ran straight into a wall of two tall senior boys.

"What the hell is that smell?" Cory asked, glaring at me, while Jeremy stood silently, brushing a hand over his scalp, clearly counting the time until this exchange could end. "Did you try another one of Mom's perfumes again?"

"I haven't done that since I was six, Cor."

Cory plugged his nose and fanned his hand in front of his face. "Seriously, what is that?"

"Tim Williams exploded something on me," I said, frowning.

"That's what she said," Jess called proudly, closing the classroom door behind her.

"Didn't that joke stop being funny like five years ago?" Jeremy asked, avoiding my eyes.

"Maybe, but, oh wow, Anna, you do stink."

Jess cringed, taking a step back.

I rolled my eyes. "I was on my way to the bathroom to clean up."

"And then you bumped into these guys. I know. I saw the whole thing while ignoring Mr. Smith's dramatic reading of 'Song of Myself.'"

"That poetry unit was boring as hell," Cory said, leaning his elbow on Jeremy's shoulder. "But hey, you know what won't be boring?"

"Good transition," Jeremy mumbled.

"This weekend! Jeremy's parents are out of town, and we're having a little early birthday celebration for our boy here on Saturday night. Why don't you two join? Anna, I'm sure you can locate a shower before then."

"If not, I have plenty at my house," Jeremy offered, biting the corner of his smirk.

"All right, then, Anna, let's go get you cleaned up," Jess jumped in. "I wish I had an extra shirt or something, but maybe we can find something in the lost and found."

"Here." Jeremy dropped his bag and slipped off his sweatshirt, offering it to me. "It's not your style, but it'll be better than smelling like rotten eggs."

I thanked him, took it from his outstretched hand, and fought the impulse to bring it up to my face to breathe in his scent.

"Jess, I mean it, you should come, even if Anna won't," Cory insisted. "I can show you around, get you the best drinks, spend some time together, you know."

She nodded, eyes squinting. "Tempting, Cor. I don't know how I'll be able to resist that offer."

"Well, what can I say?" Cory laughed, patting Jeremy on the back. "I am pretty irresistible."

Jess pulled me toward the bathroom and made no promises, even with my brother's continued insistence. I dropped my shirt into the garbage can and used a wad of wet paper towels to clean off my stomach.

"So gross. So, so gross."

"Your scent?" Jess asked. "Or your brother?"

I considered it for a second. "Both."

"Whatever, I just think it's a bummer I didn't get an invite when Jeremy's mom will be home. I've been asking you forever to get an official introduction to her. Ooh, how about I escort you back to class?"

"Gah," I yelped, rolling up the sleeves on Jeremy's peace offering. "Why have you always had a thing for Mrs. Blake?"

"Uh, you have eyes. Even if they're straight."

"It's all kinds of wrong, Jess. A little creepy, even."

She touched up her lipstick in the mirror. "I don't see it."

"She's a teacher. You're underage. And she's married."

She turned to me, crossing her arms across her chest. "I thought you didn't believe that marriage was anything more than, and I quote, an outdated social construct."

"I do, but other people don't see it that way."

"Maybe she does."

I glared at her, and we both laughed.

11

SUMMER

By August, Jeremy and I settled into a steady routine.

After I finished my tutoring and studying, and Jeremy finished his workouts, we'd lay around and watch movies, or fool around, until Cory came home. Sometimes the three of us would go out for burgers and fries. Sometimes they'd stay in. Sometimes they went out, and Jeremy would send me flirty texts and funny pictures of Cory doing something stupid.

More often than not, late at night, I'd sneak over to the pool house. On the weekends, we'd both get sucked into family activities or other obligations, but occasionally, we'd cross paths at the pool.

On the hottest Sunday of the summer, I stood on the diving platform for what felt like the hundredth time. I gave up on a lounge chair in favor of sunbathing twenty feet up until the heat became overwhelming then I'd do a trick dive in the water and climb back again, starting the process all over.

I toed the line, mentally planning out the motions of which dive I would do, and Jeremy, surrounded by his usual posse, walked in. I smiled to myself, remembering our bet on a naked dive. Part of me wished we were alone so that I could just do it now. Despite the heat, the thought of Jeremy watching that, and enjoying it, made me shiver.

Jeremy slipped off his shirt, and the sweat from this morning's run glistened on his skin. I swallowed, hoping no one below could see how my body was reacting to his, even at a distance.

One of the girls in the group glided up, asking if he could please put sunscreen on her back where she couldn't reach, and he pretended not to hear her.

Before jumping in, though, he looked up and winked at me.

In lieu of showing off, I dove in forward, wanting to meet Jeremy in the middle of the pool. I opened my eyes underwater, pushing my limbs faster to meet him in one breath. The water pounded against my ears, and I broke through that muffled underwater sound as we surfaced at the same time.

"I'm telling my family I'm heading home," I said, cutting off his protest at putting an early end to our typical game of staring at each other without trying to let on to anyone else. "Wait five minutes, then meet me in the locker room. Last shower stall on the right."

I splashed him, then used my rusty backstroke to carry me to the edge.

After grabbing my towel and purse and saying a quick goodbye to my parents, I cut indoors, dropping my stuff in an open locker. I stripped down in the shower, relaxing under the spray, and waited for Jeremy.

The door opened, and the tread of footsteps headed past the showers and over to the lockers.

A lock clicked, and after a clang open and shut, he slipped in beside me, pulling the curtain closed. He held the condom up, an easy victory wave, and I covered my mouth with his.

Urgency fueled me forward, making me eager to touch him. I untied his trunks and kneeled down. I took him in my mouth, in the recently well-practiced way that I discovered drove him crazy, and he leaned back against the tile. I peered up at him, and he locked his hands on the side of my face, holding on so he could go deeper.

I relaxed my throat, watching his mouth press into a thin line of concentration, until he drew back, pulling me upward. The steam grew around us, and I stood on my tiptoes to whisper in his ear.

"Touch me," I demanded.

I pushed his hand downward, holding it just how I wanted it, as I rocked against him until I nearly passed out.

My legs shook as I turned around, kneeling against the pull-down bench. I peered up at him, feeling insanely exposed, and the look on his face erased all of my self-consciousness.

He gaped, mouth open, and gripped my hips.

"Condom," I reminded.

He looked at me, shaking his head and grinning, then tore open the package with his teeth.

He positioned himself, and I surged my back upward.

We both cried out, too loud for this public place. I

covered my mouth with my hand, the other supporting my weight against the wall, and he bent over, licking up my spine. I trembled, and we both came together, the angle undoing us both quickly.

Jeremy pulled me back up and held me against the wall, sliding his tongue in my mouth as we both rode out the feeling.

I stepped into the stream of the water, in an attempt to tame my hair back, and he pressed the nozzle of the facility-provided soap to lather us both up.

The locker room door opened, and we both stood as still as statues.

Our eyes met in humored panic when Cory's familiar whistling carried through. He took his time to use the bathroom, wash his hands, and change for the pool.

By the time he stepped out through the back door, the water ran cold in the shower, and we both grasped at towels, wrapping up like mummies.

"Maybe we should stick to the pool house," Jeremy said, rubbing his hands down my sides to warm me up. "I do have a shower there, you know."

I wrung out my bikini, dumping it in my bag, and pulled on my loose shirt and jean shorts.

"Sometimes you need to have a little risk if you want a big reward," I said, tying my hair up in a messy bun.

I turned to see his reaction, but his face had fallen at whatever was on his phone.

"I've got to go," he said, quickly. "Dad's looking for me."

"Go first. I'll sneak out in a bit."

He nodded, slipping his shirt overhead, and placed a chaste kiss on my temple.

I promised myself I'd keep my mouth shut about Jeremy's relationship with his dad, after years of watching their tumultuous back and forth from the sidelines, but it was increasingly difficult to do so after the fundraiser.

As the summer progressed, most of our time together ended because of Mark and his expectations, and it was a huge downer.

I was growing very selfish when it came to Jeremy and the few weeks we had left until school started. Even worse, the next day, he didn't show up for our usual afternoon rendezvous.

I laid on my floor, flipping through my phone, trying not to look desperate enough to text him demanding his attention. I sent a message to Jess, but she was MIA again. She constantly blamed her phone coverage and a new love interest she'd sat next to in the sole Starbucks by her grandparents' house. She'd given me all the details of their highly caffeinated romance, and I deflected almost every question of what was happening with me. We hadn't talked since.

I closed all my apps, finding them just as boring as me, and I tapped around until I settled on the notepad. I deleted old grocery lists and scrolled past an ongoing list of movies I wanted to see, and it hit me — my original list from the beginning of summer, titled "Anna's Summer To-Do List."

I ran through it, and my lack of accomplishments spurred something panicky inside me.

I definitely didn't get a tattoo or a speeding ticket, leave the state, skinny dip, or anything else like that. If anything, I've dragged Jeremy into my lazy world, when it was supposed to be the other way around. The air escaped my lungs, and I jumped up, suddenly feeling suffocated.

I ripped off my pajamas, which I'd taken to wearing all day these days, and searched for a clean set of clothes.

"Sorry I'm late," Jeremy said, grazing right out of the box of Fruit Loops as he walked up the stairs. "And starving."

He trailed off, watching me pace across the room frantically.

I roughly pulled on shorts and a tank top, setting off in search of my wallet among the giant pile of clothes. I huffed, digging through the fabrics only to realize it was on my nightstand.

"Something wrong?"

I laughed, a little maniacally. "Nothing's wrong, Jeremy. Just a whole lot of nothing in general."

"Not this again, Anna," he pleaded. "I thought we moved past this." He set the box aside and put both arms on his head in frustration.

"I haven't done anything on my list, or on your non-list list, and it's freaking me out," I admitted. "I am — no, we are — running out of time."

He stared at me, expression stone-cold, and then started cracking up.

"Stop laughing," I said, annoyance rampant.

"No one is holding you back but yourself, Anna. When are you going to realize that? You have a flexible job, steady income, a car that you never want to drive, and endless amounts of time. So how the hell are you so angry with yourself, and everyone else, all the time?"

He was right, of course.

My anger radiated out to everyone, to myself, to the tear of frustration that formed and threatened to run hot down my cheek. I gritted my teeth.

"That's changing," I decided, sniffling once. "Right now."

I walked out of the room, and he followed me down both levels of steps. I grabbed the keys off of the shelf and pressed the button to open the garage door.

"I realize this isn't the best time for me to tell you this, but I'm blocking you in," he admitted, doing a terrible job of hiding his smile.

I shot him a look of annoyance and followed him to his car, just as Cory pulled in.

He rolled down the window. "Going somewhere?"

"Yes," I said. "And you're driving."

I slid in the front seat, relegating Jeremy to the back, and pressed the garage door closed on the receiver. Cory looked between Jeremy and me, asking a silent question with his eyes, and Jeremy just shrugged.

"Address?"

"We're going into the city," I said, sharply. "Just head south, and I'll tell you the exit."

To his credit, he nodded, turned up the music, and pressed on the gas.

I loved going to the city. It only had good memories for me — going to the theater, being dragged by my parents to the occasional baseball game, visiting colleges with Cory this spring.

There was always something magical that happened on the long stretch of road that led from our house in suburban Pennsylvania to the tall, compact buildings on the skyline, a reminder of how quickly your scenery, and your opportunity, could change.

The closer we got to the hustle of downtown, the more my mood improved, and by the time I'd directed Cory across a few bridges into the South Side, I was almost excited.

"Turn left, it's up ahead."

"Anna, a tattoo?" Jeremy asked, sliding up between us.

Cory slowed, pulling into the parking lot. "No. No way. Not happening. Mom and Dad will kill me."

He made a big turn, intending to turn around to take us home, but I put my hand on his forearm, stopping him.

"I want to get my ears pierced," I explained. "Will you sign for it?"

I put on my best innocent doe eyes, hoping that would rouse pity for his sister who was trying to conquer her fear of needles. And it worked.

He backed the car up, throwing it in park before turning the keys. "That's it, all right? No belly button. No eyebrow. Not doing that."

I threw my arms around him, surprising him with a hug, and he returned it.

We walked to the entrance, and I told them how I heard that tattoo shops were trying to get rid of the stigma with their reputation and expand their clientele.

"I also read that it's better for your body to be pierced with an actual needle than one of those cheap guns at the mall."

Jeremy ran a hand through his curls. "Well, you could always do what Cory tried to do when we were fourteen, pierce your ear with a stapler during library time."

"Hard pass on that one," I said, the thought of the blood all over his shirt when he came home that day made me a little queasy.

We stepped in, and I spoke with the receptionist, who stared at Cory and Jeremy. She merely nodded along as I talked to her, eyeing the boys who were checking out the earrings and other items for sale along the wall behind me.

"Are there forms or something I need my legal guardian to sign?" I asked, gently.

She opened a drawer, pulling out the consent form and a pen, which I handed over to Cory, who scanned the document quickly and scribbled his signature at the bottom. I passed it back, and the woman led me to the room with Cory and Jeremy trailing close.

"I just can't believe you've never had your ears pierced," Cory said. "Isn't that some sort of rite of passage for every twelve-year-old girl?"

"My own brother doesn't know this about me," I sighed. Jeremy, who had become very familiar with the state of my earlobes as of late, kept his mouth shut. "I've always been terrified of it getting caught in my hair. Those dangly ones, you know, getting all mixed up?"

We were guided to a small room, where a woman with buzzed black hair, tattoos, gauged earlobes, and the trendiest glasses I'd ever seen, was disinfecting her weapons of choice.

She glanced back at us. "Who's getting pierced?" I raised my hand. "One of you boys, out."

My eyes flashed to Jeremy, who raised his eyebrows at Cory.

"This is all you, man," Cory said, hands up. "Just yell for me if she passes out."

"I'm Amber, and I'll be piercing you today. Ears, right? First time?"

I nodded, taking a seat on the padded table. It kind of reminded me of a doctor's office setup, now that I really looked, except instead of pastel walls and pictures of fish, there were velvet accents and spray painted decorations.

"So first I'll mark your ears, and you can check the placement in the mirror. Once you give me the thumbs up, I'll put the clamp down, stick a needle through it, put the stud in, and repeat on the other side. About forty-five seconds total, and you're done."

"That's it?" I asked, less nervous now than when she started her spiel.

"That's it."

"Okay, I'm ready."

"Which earrings did you pick?"

"I was supposed to pick?"

Jeremy cleared his throat. "I found a good pair."

I nodded, and he stepped out to grab them from the display case as Amber put the cold, eye-hole clamp on my lobe on the agreed placement. I closed my eyes, and she did a quick sterilization on the earrings, talking me through the process.

I reached for Jeremy's hand, and he held it tightly, as if I was preparing for brain surgery instead of getting my ears pierced.

"Okay, breathe in and out." On the exhale, a pinch. "Great job. Once more." Again, I breathed out, and a quick pinch, followed up a tug, which hurt worse than the actual needle. "All done," Amber said, tossing her gloves in the trash.

"How do they look?"

"Perfect as usual," he promised, handing me the mirror so I could check for myself.

The tiniest, most delicate silver flowers were now punched through my ears.

"Wow. I love them!" I jumped up and kissed Jeremy. "Thank you for picking these out." I turned to Amber. "And thank you for piercing them!"

She laughed, running me quickly through aftercare, and waved us back to the front.

I held my hair back for Cory to see, and he stepped back from the receptionist, who tried her best attempt to hold his attention, to applaud my bravery.

"How much do I owe?" I pulled out my wallet, but Cory shook his head.

"Already paid and tipped," he said, eyeing the receptionist. "Let's go find some food."

To show my gratitude, I treated them both to an early dinner, hitting up one of Cory's favorite places in the city, a hole in the wall with the best wings not too far away from the way home.

The ride back much better than the ride in, the music turned down in favor of talking and laughing. Cory and I stayed in the car as Jeremy backed out of the driveway, nodding to both of us.

As we pulled into the garage, I felt a sense of foreboding when Cory slowly turned off the car.

Part of me wanted to run like hell, but I sat back waiting for whatever was coming.

He cleared his throat and tapped on the steering wheel. "I wanted to talk to you about Jeremy."

I opened and closed my mouth several times, wondering if he saw our post-pierce kiss.

"What's there to talk about?" I settled on, fishing to see what he would say.

"I know there is something going on between you," he said, rubbing his thumbs at his temples. "I may not be as smart as you, but I'm not a complete dumbass."

I shifted nervously, wanting to deflect the overbearing older brother speech. "Cory, I'm fine. I don't need you to protect me from your best friend."

"It's not you that I'm looking out for. It's him." He scratched his jaw. "Jeremy has been infatuated with you forever." He looked sideways to confirm his suspicion. "I knew you had no idea. God, you're so unaware sometimes, Anna."

I couldn't hide my look of surprise.

"I see the way he looks at you now. It's less and less guarded, and that worries me."

"Worries you? How?" I held my arms protectively over my chest as my mind raced.

He turned to me, his eyes full of pity. "Because I don't think you're good enough for him."

I was speechless. The only sign I registered what he said were the tears that gathered in my eyes. The side view mirror reflected the red rims right back to me.

"Jeremy is the best guy in the world, like the best brother I could have wished for."

"I'm your sister," I reminded him through a clenched jaw.

"But we're so different, Anna. I've always been more like him than like you. You're calculated, and you wear your intelligence like a suit of armor, and I kind of love that Jeremy has found a way to break through it. That edge to you, though, where you box people out, it's cruel as hell, and he doesn't deserve that."

He stared me down, but I refused to meet his gaze.

"I can't help but feel like you're an inch from running away from everything. You already know the crap he has to deal with at home, the pressure he feels crushed under, and I just think that if you're not in it for the long haul, to really be with him long-term, then I can't help but wonder what the hell you're doing."

I turned to face my brother, his face paled at the harsh words that he let out of his mouth.

"I just wish you could find a way to let yourself be happy, Anna."

"Me too," I mumbled.

He breathed out and left me alone in his car, with my thoughts and sobs that wracked my body until it hurt.

12

FALL

My mother and I sat in the square, windowless room in silence.

The chairs were so uncomfortable, squeaking with even the slightest movement, that I wondered if it was on purpose, to encourage conversations to be short.

She offered me a small smile and a nod of encouragement, and I huffed, crossing my arms.

"Sorry about that, the printer was acting up," Mr. Reeves said, shaking my mother's hand. "Sharon, nice to see on you a matter that doesn't involve trying to get your son out of a suspension."

I laughed, remembering how Jeremy and Cory glued about fifty dollars in change on the school floors in a bunch of classrooms and the hallways as a prank, and my mother shot me a warning look to pull myself together.

"I really appreciate your time, Ken. I thought it would be a good idea for the three of us to sit down and discuss Anna's future."

I rolled my eyes, adjusting myself in the chair to the tune of grinding metal and an oversized clock ticking on the wall.

Despite her assurance that my future was up to me, had I been given the choice, I would not be sitting here in this stuffy office.

Mr. Reeves reviewed my transcript and academic file with the two of us, complimenting me on my high grade point average and test scores, and my mother beamed with pride.

"I have to be honest with you, Anna. Schools will be impressed by your numbers, but what stands out after more than thirty seconds of looking at your file is how light it is."

"What do you mean?" I asked. "I assumed admissions counselors didn't want stacks of papers detailing any trouble I'd started in high school."

"Which there is none," my mother reminded him as if that wasn't obvious.

"You have an alarming lack of extracurricular activities." He licked his finger, inciting a cringe from both my mother and me, to flip through the notes. "You've managed to quit every single thing you started including, let's see, painting scenery for the school play, self-defense classes, debate team, cross country."

"She made me try running," I deflected, pointing at my mom. "I gave up after a mile and walked straight to Dairy Queen from the trail."

He ignored me. "It says here that you helped out on Jessica Lewis' successful campaign to run for class president your freshman year. Did you enjoy that?"

My major contribution to that was to do Cory's chores for a week so that he and Jeremy, cool older sophomores at the time, would put in a good word with all the freshman boys to vote for her. It worked, though. She won in a landslide.

I shrugged, tapping my foot on the thirty-year-old carpet.

My mom sniffled beside me, accepting a tissue from Mr. Reeves to wipe her tears.

"Mom," I said, tentatively. "Are you all right?"

She laughed, the way people do when the tears fall even though the timing is completely inappropriate.

"It's just hard to hear that your daughter isn't reaching her full potential. You're so smart, Anna, but your dad and I just wonder what we did wrong, and we're at a loss of how to help you. And that's awful for anyone, but especially for two parents who love you as much as your dad and I do."

"You didn't do anything wrong, Mom," I promised. "I guess I'm just pickier than Cory, and I know it's frustrating, but I think it's okay."

The waterworks started up again, and I sighed.

"Mom, pull it together. We're going to be fine. Poor Mr. Reeves doesn't need to see this. He's a district employee, not a shrink."

"Well actually," he cut in, "I have a master's degree in psychology and a doctorate in school counseling."

My mouth dropped open.

"But let's get back on track here, in the interest of time. Anna, you're at the point where you need to do some soul-searching. Take the time to really think through your options. Do the research as to what appeals to you, explore locations as well as areas of interest then make yourself a list."

"I already have a list," I admitted.

My mother gasped in pleasant surprise. "What are you considering? One of the Ivy Leagues? USC? Maybe something a little closer to home?"

My stomach dropped, and I felt stupid.

She'd be embarrassed if I admitted that my list was more about California rolls than colleges in that state, and I didn't want her to start crying again.

"You don't have to tell us now," Mr. Reeves jumped in. "I'd also urge you to consider a trade school, where you could learn skills that you could apply to a job after earning a degree."

"Like how some students leave school early to learn to be mechanics and cooks?"

He nodded. "There are all sorts of programs where you could start earning college credit next year, taking classes on technology, development, entrepreneurship, food science, you name it."

I mulled it over, wondering if a practical application would be the best way to approach my indecision.

Seeing for the first time I showed interest in something, he added quickly, "Let me grab you some more information on those for you to consider."

My mom and I were alone again, and she turned to me, saying nothing, but how she grabbed my hand and squeezed it tight, I knew she was grasping at a little bit of hope.

And maybe I was, too.

13

SUMMER

I AVOIDED Jeremy for the next few days, texting him with half-true excuses, and made sure to leave my house during times I assumed he'd be around.

The first day, I was at a loss of what to do and ended up sitting in the parking lot outside of the dollar store for hours, listening to music on shuffle.

After that, I found a purpose — crossing as many things off of my official summer to-do list that Jeremy jokingly forbid me from utilizing, embarrassed that I hadn't thought of it sooner.

It felt a little strange, to be honest.

I took myself out to a restaurant to try sushi for the first time, drove across the border to Ohio for the hell of it and took a picture of the welcome sign, bought temporary tattoos from a gumball machine, spent an afternoon at Kennywood, and finally, in the dead of night when everyone was asleep, I shotgunned a beer in my backyard.

The distractions worked a little bit.

It was a luxury to have my mind so focused on a task, but I felt like half a person without Jeremy.

I discovered I missed him in the moments when I was happiest, wishing he was there to share it with me. But then I kept thinking about what Cory said, how strongly he must feel about me, about who I am, if he had to stage an intervention.

Cory's words were sharp, a knife in the stomach, but I deserved it.

Jeremy and I went deeper than I planned in that fleeting moment of rebelliousness in the kitchen.

At some point, we stopped being a little summer game, diving off the high dive and never resurfacing. I felt empty, thinking of how I allowed my resolve to waver, my feelings to grow, and I needed to figure out how to move forward.

The way I saw it, I had two options: follow Cory's advice and rip the Band-Aid off or go along with the charade for an undetermined amount of time, the light at the end of the tunnel growing more and more narrow until I died from asphyxiation.

I chose option three: Delay the inevitable.

Until Jeremy tracked me down. Not that it was difficult.

I stood in the pantry and stared at the calendar that my mom had pinned to the door, keeping track of all the events, games, and birthdays we were responsible for acknowledging. I stared at the box highlighted in red, the first day of school, this coming Tuesday.

Pulling out a bag of marshmallows and a box of Rice Krispies, I propped open the fridge to grab the butter then got to work.

The rich smell of delicious, warmed fat and sugar

filled the air, and my mouth watered as I poured in the dry cereal.

The front door sounded, and I wasn't surprised to see Jeremy hanging against the counter shortly after, arms crossed across his chest.

"Does it seem a little sacrilegious to you? Changing the makeup of your favorite food?"

I scooped the mixture into the lined baking sheet, dropping a few extra marshmallows on top.

"I guess it's the same as putting them in milk, just more fun to eat," I said, somewhat lifelessly. "In the past, I've added other cereals and chocolate chips, but I was in the mood for the original."

"There's a career idea for you, Anna. If anyone asks, just tell them you're already the world's first cereal chef."

I glared at him.

"Better than a serial killer, which is how you're looking at me right now."

"Somehow I don't think choosing a career path based on my interests at age seventeen is the brightest idea."

"Most people do it," he reminded me, stepping over to gently pull my hair back and check on my piercings.

He kissed my temple, and I pretended the gesture meant nothing to me.

"My only three hobbies are eating sugar, watching action movies, and you, Jeremy. That doesn't exactly sound like a future, does it?" He moved his hand toward the pan, and I covered the dish. "It needs to set for a few minutes."

I looked up at him, surprised to see his face was slightly red, his eyebrow dipping down with nervousness.

He pulled a chair out at the kitchen table, gesturing for

me to join him. "Anna, I wanted to talk to you about something."

I collapsed into a chair across from him, and he brushed past my edginess, distracted with whatever he was about to say.

"I talked to my dad," he said slowly. "About everything."

Selfishly, I wondered if that "everything" included us because of course my first thought went to how it affected me. I could hear Cory's voice in my head, disappointed. I shook it off.

"My mom and I had kind of an intervention after the scene at the fundraiser, and he was better for a little while, but it's bad again. He just always gets so damn angry, and it's much worse when he is drunk, which is all the time. So yesterday, I showed up to his office after he finished up with patients for the day. I figured if he was in his professional mindset, he'd have a better chance of hearing what I said."

My heart ached for him, and every part of me ached to touch him, but I held back.

"It was awful," he said, pinching the bridge of his nose. "He got defensive, and then he got combative. I stayed for hours, repeating the same things over again, but it was like talking to a wall. He tried to leave until I told him I was quitting basketball."

I gasped, and he smiled ruefully. "That shut him up."

"You're quitting?"

"Not yet. I want to play this year, my final one, just for me."

"That's great," I said, quietly. "Really great for you,

Jeremy."

"And then things got emotional. Everything else kind of spilled out about how his drinking was impacting Mom and I, and I think he really heard me this time." He bit his lip. "We'll see, I guess. Take it day by day and see how it goes."

I pulled my foot up to the chair, resting my chin against my knee. "I'm really proud of you. That took a lot of courage."

"I couldn't have done it without you, Anna."

"What? Why?"

He took my limp hand in his, tracing the lines of my palms. "Something about us, this summer, just gave me the boost. Or at least got me thinking about the future enough to make a change to it."

I pulled my hand away, hard enough to surprise him.

"Jeremy, don't," I warned.

"Anna, I love you," he said, simply.

"No."

"No?"

"You don't love me," I told him as calmly as I could. "You love the thought of me. The idea of falling for the girl you grew up with who you watched learn how to ride a bike. The girl who was almost always emotionally unavailable, a challenge instead of the girl who kept things light and easy. The girl who your parents love. The girl who fits easily into your life. And it's not me."

His eyes were wide, his lips thin. "Why are you fighting me so hard, Anna?"

"Say we stay together. Let's say we tell all of our family, and they're just so overjoyed to be tied together. We go to college in the city. We move in together. You get an internship your senior year and it turns into a steady job. I'm ridiculously unhappy because I never found myself, I just stayed within an hour drive of these cookie-cutter houses and people. I grow to resent you, and your career, and our children who cry all the time. We become distant, but we stay together for the kids, and then twenty years go by, and we're middle-aged, overweight, and starting all over again."

"So you've thought about it, then?"

"That's how our life would go, and I don't want any part of it."

"Who says that's how our life would go?"

"Okay, here's this one, what if you meet someone at a party next year? What if you grow to hate me because I ruined your college years? What if being in a relationship holds you back from getting wild? Excessive drinking and sleeping around?"

He laughed. "I've spent the past three years messing around, dead sober. I'm not going to pick up a binge-drinking habit after all the shit with my dad. Are you even trying to use logic and reasoning for this? Or are you just making excuses because you're scared?"

"The fact that you're saying it is 'logic' means that it is rooted in actual logic. You just don't recognize it as valid because it's not what you want." I put my hands on my head in frustration. "This is useless. You're going to have a comeback for everything I say."

"I usually do. That's how conversations work, Anna."

"This isn't a conversation. This is an end."

He stared at me.

"Jeremy, I don't know how to say this, so I'm just going to say it. My life is going to be so much more than this. I'm going to do more than be the girl who fell for the captain of the basketball team in high school, who gave away her future to get married and stay in her hometown."

He laughed. "I'm not asking you for any of those things."

"But—"

"More importantly, I would never ask you to give up anything that you want to do. I just want to be a part of you doing it, to help you figure it out, even, just like you've helped me."

"Don't you see that's the next step of all of this? And the steps after?"

"I don't."

"I mean, hell, Jeremy, look at your dad. He has everything he could ever want, and he still needs to look down a bottle until he can't stand."

That one hurt, I could tell. It was like punching myself in the stomach, seeing the look on his face.

He smiled, sadly. "I love you, Anna Wright. I want to be with you for longer for this summer, for the future. I know you feel the same way. I feel it so clearly, just like I feel how frightened you are."

I chewed the inside of my cheek. "I don't want this, Jeremy. You're feeling rejection, not second-guessing from me. I may not know where I will be in a year, and it's scary as hell to think about what comes after that, but I want to end things with you, here and now, at the end of summer like we agreed to."

"I never agreed to that."

He stood up, bracing himself on the back of the chair. His back muscles, ones I could pick out of a lineup with my eyes closed, were tense, almost cat-like. His eyes pleaded with me.

"This is what life is, Anna," he cried. "It's not some big, radical experiment. It's about the people you're with and who you value. You can say you want to change, but the truth is, if you don't move forward, I can't fix it for you."

I slammed my hands on the table, making him jump for once. "I don't want you to fucking fix me, Jeremy."

"Things don't have to be this difficult," he exhaled, deflated. "Everything can continue on as it was. The only difference would be that I'd walk you to class and occasionally try to make-out with you in the stairwell. That's it, the first step, not the big scary future you mapped out for us."

He straightened up, watching me mull over his words.

"And you'd come to my games."

"I already come to your games," I admitted quietly.

"Because sometimes it's the only thing to do on a Friday night or our parents drag you. I'm talking about being there to watch me, and people would know that was why you came. They'd know about us."

He prepared for whatever excuse I would lay out for him to tear apart, and I couldn't do it.

I brought my hands up to my mouth, holding back all of the emotion I could. I started shaking my head and then the tears poured out.

"I'm sorry," I nearly choked. "I can't."

Frustration crossed his features, and without another glance, he walked out.

14

FALL

"Should we ring the doorbell?" I asked, already regretting letting Jess talk me into wearing a long-sleeved crop top.

I pulled it down, trying to cover up another inch of my midriff, and she smacked my hand.

"Stop fidgeting! I kind of hate how good you look in blue."

She popped a piece of gum in her mouth, sticking the wrapper in her knee-high boot.

Jess was one of those people who let random bits of paper trash accumulate in her purse, her room, and her car. It drove me crazy, and I was usually the one who broke down and ended up cleaning out everything.

She stuck her face up against the translucent glass that framed the door, trying to see inside the house.

"How did you used to come by this summer? Just stroll in like you own the place? March right up to his hot mom and talk me up?"

I rolled my eyes. "I used to sneak into the pool house in the back." I pointed out the hedges around the side of the house.

"Well, we're definitely not doing that," she decided, smoothing down her skirt. "Nature and I, we don't really get along these days."

"I'd hardly call expensively landscaped yards 'nature,' Jess."

"Well I'm still scarred from gardening this summer, so we're going in the normal way."

She reached over to turn the knob, but it opened before her hand hit the brass circle.

"Hey," Jeremy said, swinging it open. "You made it."

He glanced at Jess, nodding, and over to me, where his eyes moved over my outfit and exposed skin in a way that rendered me speechless.

Jess smacked her gum, gaze darting between us, and she used both hands to flip her hair back.

"Thanks for the invite, Jeremy," she said, cocking her hip. "Well, actually, I guess we have Cory to thank because you technically didn't invite us, but seeing as it is your house, I still wanted to be polite. Anyway, is your mom home?"

He raised an eyebrow. "Class question?"

"More like ass question," she said, low enough for me to hear.

I elbowed her in the ribs.

"She and my dad are having a weekend away together," he explained. "Hence Cory's desire to throw a party in my house that I'm definitely going to be stuck cleaning up."

"Oh right," she said, casually. "Your early birthday celebration. Well, we didn't get you anything except for our presence, so you're welcome. I guess?"

He opened the door a little wider so we could slip in, and Jess pushed her way past him.

"I'm getting a drink," she announced, her heeled boots clicking down the hall toward the blaring music. "Wow," she said silently from behind Jeremy's back, eyes wide gesturing to the inside of the house.

The high ceilings seemed exceptionally drafty, covered in a fresh coat of white paint, and a chandelier of Edison bulbs created an interesting hue. The dual staircases, where Jeremy, Cory, and I once had a Slinky race, were refinished with a dark, almost black, stain, flanked by iron railings.

Jeremy walked beside me as I detoured through one of the side rooms, stopping at a wall of pictures. They were those expensive kinds of frames, where there was more glass than a picture, and they all matched — something never to be seen in my house.

Jeremy was the clear star of the photos, and Cory was a regular presence, but I was surprised to find myself, at various ages, in at least five of them.

I hovered over one in particular that my mom had taken at the old drive-in, which was torn down a few years ago. I was pretty sure it was a fast food place now. Cory, Jeremy, and I camped out on the bed of my dad's truck, me in between them.

To anyone else's eyes, our setup looked innocent enough to not give a second glance, but I stared at it, and my stomach dropped.

I traced Cory, staring over the camera lens at the

screen, mouth open in shock at whatever happened in the movie. My finger smudged the glass as I moved toward me, ten years ago, smiling like I'd never been so excited to be somewhere in my entire life, holding one side of a Twizzlers package, as Jeremy held the other, turned completely toward me with a look of admiration I would never have believed a seven-year-old was capable of until this moment.

I swallowed, facing the real-life Jeremy, and I was at a loss for words.

His expression was careful, but I saw through it, almost as if I could look directly into his heart and see what he'd tried to show me months ago.

"Look, Jeremy," I started. "I—"

"I don't believe it!" My brother yelled, and the moment between us completely shattered. Cory's beer spilled over onto the floor, enticing a groan from Jeremy. He threw his arm around me, dragging me into the party. "She's finally slumming it with us."

Jess, who had made her way through three Jell-o shots, snickered at my expense.

I tried to push Cory off, but he gripped me harder, steering into the party to reintroduce me to the same people who I've known but mostly avoided for years. Kim Patterson, to her credit, said nothing at all to me as I stood in the same circle as her. He slurred through conversations for at least an hour then somehow persuaded a few of us into playing a round of Kings. I grabbed Jess and a bag of Chex Mix, the only cereal-containing snack I'd found in his kitchen.

The three of us, along with some of Jeremy's teammates, whose names I memorized this time around — Mitch, Keith, and Brent — sat in a circle, as Cory drunkenly explained the rules.

"And ace means water full, no, waterfall, and you have to start chugging and can't stop until the person next to you does."

I pulled up my phone, checking his explanation against the rules on some drinking game website, and it matched up.

"So there's no way to win?" I asked. "You just get drunk?"

"Pretty much, yeah," Mitch said, bringing everyone in for a round of cheers.

I laughed, taking a drink.

While I'd never really ever drank, aside from sips of champagne at special occasions, shotgunning that beer this summer made me feel powerful and just tipsy enough to create an appreciation for the stale-tasting liquid. When cold, it wasn't really that bad.

Brent dropped an unopened can in the middle of us. "So after you draw your card, you have to stick it under the tab. And if you're the one who opens it—"

"You have to be the one to chug it as fast as you can, sucking down humiliation, empty calories, and a guaranteed hangover?" Jess finished, twisting her finger around the seal of another green-colored shot.

"Pretty much, yeah," Mitch said again, bringing everyone in for yet another round cheers.

We all took turns pulling cards, assigning drinks, and making up rules, and I had to admit, it was actually a lot of fun.

A few rounds in, the guys had all picked me to be their mate, which pretty much guaranteed me a sip at every turn. Some people sat on the leather couches, mildly interested in the outcome, but others paired off and escaped upstairs, no doubt about to play a different kind of game.

I pulled a queen, which meant we had to ask questions until someone answered one by mistake. "Keith, who's the drunkest here?"

"Is it you, Miss Jessica?"

"Are you accusing me of not being able to hold my liquor?"

"Cory?" Jeremy called from the front door.

"Jeremy!" Cory screamed, and we all erupted into laughter.

"You lose!" Jess pointed at him. "You didn't ask a question."

He stood up, taking a large drink and bowing to us, and turned to see the receptionist from the tattoo place and Amber, the woman who shoved needles through my earlobes.

"Phoebe and Amber stopped by to say hi."

He said it so casually, I was terrified this was a regular occurrence for them, double dates that I'd accidentally set up. I didn't dare ask about that, but I found a way around it.

"Cory, what about Kathleen?"

He shrugged as if he hadn't worked all summer to get her out with him. "What about her?" He strode over, offering his arm to Phoebe, who nodded at me in passing.

"Yeah, what about her?" Jess asked, eyeing Amber with

interest who, along with Jeremy, followed my brother outside.

Cory led them over to the fire pit, a large circle in the middle of their concrete patio. He pointed vaguely to their wood-fired pizza oven, and I remembered being terrified of it when I was little. Mark and Alicia had invited our family over to try it the weekend after the brick set, and I screamed, scared I was going to get thrown into the opening and burned to death for being bad. It was a gruesome thought for a five-year-old, but it was met with tears of laughter by the adults, which only made me fall into hysterics.

By the way everyone turned to look at me, I was willing to bet that was the story Cory just shared.

"Five! Guys, we drink," Mitch laughed, pulling me back into the game. "And my mate, Anna!"

I groaned. "I'm out of beer again," I said, as Brent put a fresh can in my hand. "Funny how I never seem to be empty, actually."

I leaned forward on all fours, pulling a card.

"King! Yes!"

Jess was the last one to pull a king, forcing everyone to put the cards under the middle beer can with their teeth, which was hilarious in its own right, but as the new ruler, I insisted that everyone speak with an English accent.

The results were awesomely terrible.

"Aye, mate, mind handing me a card facedown?" Keith asked, sounding more Australian-Irish than cockney.

Mitch mimicked drinking a cup of tea with his beer can, pinky out and everything. "Your accent is terrible dude," he said, barely with a twang.

"King says you must drink for that poor effort, sir," I said, channeling an inner female version of James Bond.

He sighed, taking a sip, and flipped over a jack.

This was the first time we'd landed on a "never have I ever" card, and I immediately got nervous, fearful of the three dirty male minds beside me. Mitch leaned forward, with his teeth even though he no longer had to, and slipped the card under the tab.

It popped, and we all screamed, yelling at him to chug.

I was laughing and living in the moment.

It was the happiest I'd felt in a long time, and I reached back, for Jeremy's hand, glad to share this with him. I fell to the carpet with a thud, and I remembered, painfully, that we weren't together. Like, together in the relationship sense but also in the same room.

I looked up, watching him with the crowd outside, and it made me sad.

I sprawled out on the carpet, making my own version of a snow angel, and Jess crawled over, giggling. We laid there together, and she hooked her foot around mine. I swallowed, and my world spun on its head, and I realized it wasn't from the alcohol.

She rolled over on her stomach, propped up on her elbows.

"What are you thinking about?" Jess asked, blowing a small bubble then crunching it up in her mouth.

"I made a huge mistake," I admitted.

Jess closed one eye, attempting to assess my sobriety. "Is this the alcohol talking?"

Through the windows, I watched him for a little while longer.

He went through the motions, engaging in the conversation, playing life of the party as my brother hit on an enamored Phoebe, and hugging some of his friends as they snuck in through the back, but I saw right through it.

For every smile, there was a crinkle of sadness in his eyes. For every pat on the back, there was a cross of his arms. For every cheer with his water bottle, there was a grimace at condoning his friends. For every summer, there was a fall, and I really hated wearing scarves.

I sat up suddenly, and Jess was right there with me.

"I think that," I said, starting to really panic, "I'm ready to admit that I'm an idiot."

She nodded, confirming she'd been waiting for some time for me to come to this realization. "Go outside and get your boy back."

"I might have a better idea."

15

FALL

I COULD HAVE KILLED Jessica Lewis. Murdered her in cold blood and felt no remorse.

If you aren't in this car within the next 3 minutes, I swear I'm leaving without you.

Chill.

For being the most talkative human in the entire world, she'd really mastered the art of the short text message.

I checked the clock for the hundredth time, mentally calculating that I'd missed the first quarter just by sitting here, waiting on my best friend.

"Sorry, sorry, I know you're mad, but I had an emergency," Jess said, climbing into the car. "Like real issues, Anna. You wouldn't even begin to understand it."

I glared at her, fully expecting her to launch into a tirade about her hair not setting right or how she broke off one of her claws and was out of nail glue, but after one look at my expression, she promptly shut her mouth.

The second she buckled in, my foot was on the gas, zooming through the back roads that led to the high school. Of course, the parking lot was packed, and I had to loop around twice before I gave up and created my own spot near the grass.

"Wait," Jess said, pulling on my arm before I stepped out. "Do you need, I don't know, like a pep talk or something? I mean, you're about to put yourself out there for him, which you're probably going to hate every second of, but he's going to absolutely love it, or you know, he could reject you in front of everyone. Ouch, that actually really sucks since your parents and his extended family are going to be there tonight."

"That was a fantastic pep talk, Jess, thank you," I said, slamming the door shut. "I feel so much better now."

She skipped beside me, and I pressed the button to lock the car. "Anything else I can do to help? Oh, I know. You get us seats. Like, the perfect ones where you two can lock eyes for the game, and I'll raid the concession stand."

We idled by the entrance, and I turned, grabbing onto her.

"Okay, I need you to tell me the truth because I'm only going to ask you this once and then we're going to move on because I don't want you stuck in makeover mode." I held out my arms. "Do I look okay?"

She walked around in a circle, eyeing me up and down. I wore dark blue skinny jeans, tucked into ankle boots, and Jeremy's oversized basketball hoodie. My hair was down in loose waves, but I'd used bobby pins to secure it back, showing off the earrings Jeremy picked out for me. Jess stood toe to toe and before I could stop her, she licked her thumb and dragged it below my left eyelid.

"I don't know when you're going to start taking my waterproof eyeliner suggestions seriously, but it should have been like at least an hour ago," she said, stepping back to make sure it was even. "And now, you are perfect. A more gorgeous human on a mission to get her man back does not exist in this world."

I nodded, a wordless act of gratitude, and we went in to buy our tickets.

It was crowded, way more people showed up than I expected, but apparently, the other team bussed a bunch of fans from their side in.

It was the official kickoff of the season, and I learned it was a tradition to replay the two teams from last year's state final, with the loser getting home-court advantage. I couldn't believe these people took a coach bus all the way from Philadelphia for thirty-two minutes of gameplay, but it made our team look great to scouts to have a photo in the newspaper with packed stands.

Jess, as promised, went off to wait in line for snacks, and I set off to find somewhere to sit. From the propped open door, I saw the student section was completely full, and there were sparingly few seats available elsewhere. I locked in on space big enough for her and me a few rows behind our bench.

With three minutes left in the first half, the score was tied. I walked into the gym, and the loud roar of the fans quieted slightly. Jeremy stood at the foul line, deep in concentration. I stepped sideways, behind the line of photographers crouched out of bounds, toward the open seats.

Jeremy dribbled, bending his knees slightly. He moved his gaze up toward the basket, right as I walked behind it, and he stopped.

Our eyes locked. He revealed nothing, but I mentally screamed, "Yes!!! I'm here for you!!! I want everyone to know it!!!"

His gaze dropped to my hoodie, and I turned backward, patting the number eleven. It was the number he chose when he first put on a jersey at age six, the fabric entirely too long for him at the time. I hoped he understood the message, but his eyes moved back, focusing on the ball, which swooshed through the net with ease.

Thunderous applause broke out, and I scurried to take the spot in the stands before someone else did.

With thirty seconds left in the half, we were up by six points, and Jess finally found me. Her arms were too full to check her phone, where a message from me detailing my location sat unread, and she thumped down next to me without an ounce of gracefulness.

I rejected her offer for popcorn as Jeremy passed Mitch the ball, going for an easy layup but missing, only for Keith to grab the rebound, turn around, and make the shot. Jess handed me a bag of Swedish Fish, and it sat unopened in my hand as the clock wound down to zero. She waved a Golden Grahams cereal bar in my face, and I snatched it from her so she'd stop trying to force-feed me.

"You're either super pissed at me, or you've got it bad for him," Jess insisted, unwrapping an off-brand lollipop. "Or both, you know, it can be both at the same time."

"It's a game, Jess. Some people actually come to watch them."

She scrunched up her nose. "So when are you going to talk to him?"

Jeremy returned to the bench briefly but threw a towel over his head, shielding himself from distraction. Brent handed him a water bottle as they hit the locker room for their ten-minute break, and the stands emptied slightly.

"I guess after the game?" I said, taking a handful of Skittles from her. "He saw me, though, and I can't tell if he was happy about it or not."

"If I had to guess, he was trying to fight his desperate need to haul you into the locker room for a timeout. You know, you could dribble his balls and stuff."

"Jess, you're absurd."

She fell into a fit of laughter, and I shook my head, half amused. "Pass between his legs. Take it back to the basket. Hit the rim."

"Where did you learn all of those phrases?"

She crunched the cherry flavor right off the stick. "I had to do something while I was waiting in line, and I really am glad I got the chance to use them on you right now. Your face is kind of horrified in the most hilarious way."

My phone vibrated, and I inhaled, blood coursing through my veins. I slid my thumb, only to sigh, reading Cory's name.

We're all at the game, not too late to join.

I looked up at him, surrounded by our parents and Jeremy's family. They were all animatedly talking, with

Mark the most passionate, but by all appearances sober, as he broke down the first half for Jeremy's cousins.

Twenty rows ahead of you, toward the middle.

Jess and I waved at him, and he motioned about how crowded it was.

We're fine here anyway.

Did you see Jeremy almost knock out that point guard? Jackson something from the other team.

No?

Dirtbag has been saying shit to him all game. Trying to get him riled up.

Wow.

He's just pissed because Jeremy played so well against him last year.

I didn't know what to say to that, so I looked at Cory and shrugged as both teams stepped back on the court, tossing their warm-up shirts on the bench, and the second half began with the other team having possession.

Time flew by as each team fought for the lead, and the points barely crept up. It was one of those close back-and-forth games, and I spent half the time a tense, silent mess and the other clapping like a lunatic.

Jess was even moderately entertained by the whole thing.

Once Cory pointed it out, the uncalled fouls and trash talk from Jackson were almost impossible to unsee, but Jeremy stayed focused, not even bothering to argue with the refs about missed calls. Keith took an elbow to the face from someone. He sat out until it stopped bleeding, and I had to hide my head in my hands until Jess promised me it was cleaned up.

As these types of games typically unfolded, it came down to the last ten seconds.

Jackson made two free throws, putting us two points behind. Mitch tore down the court, bringing the ball easily within feet of shooting range, only to get lost in a double team. He stepped, slightly, resigning to the fact that his shot would get blocked, and with four seconds left, he passed to Jeremy, who sprinted just outside the three-point line.

Every single person sat on the edge of their seat, holding their breath, but I stood up, covering my mouth with my hands.

The red numbers on the clock worked down to zero, a blinking reminder that time was almost up.

Jeremy crouched low, staring directly into the eyes of Jackson, whose words were foamy venom spitting from his mouth. The other coaches screamed at him to go for the foul, but he shook his head and called back obscenities. Jeremy dribbled the ball under his leg, catching it effortlessly with his other hand.

He surged forward with two steps and released, not even looking at the basket or his teammates or the opponent in front of him with the shot in the air. He smiled and craned his neck sideways to meet my eyes.

The buzzer sounded, and I saw the change within him, and within me, the realization that everything else was a game of background noise, except for us.

Everyone rushed the floor, screaming in excitement, but Jeremy and I were lost to all of that. We moved toward each other, dodging the thrashing arms and random hugs. He slipped by his teammates, who were all tackling each other and chanting, and met me, halfway between the stands and center court.

In one of our most intimate moments last summer, he told me to let go of everything, and I was so up in my own head, I couldn't comprehend what he truly meant. I needed to stop making excuses, to give up all of the self-inflicted misery, and to just be who I was with him, living in that moment. I was ready to do that now.

I threw my arms around his neck, and his hands locked at my waist.

Without a second of hesitation, I pulled him down to me, kissing him with so much need it almost hurt to be in such a public place. His mouth covered mine, and I fell into him. Every cell in my body pleaded to never go so long without this feeling again.

He broke the kiss and held his fingers against my face, shaking his head in disbelief.

I pulled back, reaching into the front pocket of his hoodie to pull out a now-crumpled piece of paper. He unfolded it, and I watched the smile hit his lips as he registered the words.

"Anna and Jeremy's Extended Summer, the officially not official list to triumph over all non-list lists," he read aloud. "Visit the Kellogg store in New York City, dive naked off of the diving platform, study journalism, find life direction, travel to Europe—"

"It's just the start of something," I cut him off. "Something that is very much not nothing."

"That's all I needed to hear," he said, catching my lips with his again.

It couldn't have just been excitement about winning the first game of the season, I realized, as another round of roars and clapping began. All of the people in the stands, including our family and friends, cheered for us.

ACKNOWLEDGMENTS

I've said it before, but I'll say it again: Writing is a lonely, beautiful, and occasionally soul-crushing practice. And while the act of putting a book together can be all of those things at once, I'm so grateful to have many amazing supporters and active participants in making this stuff go.

As a professional writer, it's a little embarrassing that I have trouble putting into words how amazing my friends and family are, but I will say that your virtual hugs, dollars spent on my work, and free publicity make me weep. Thank you for all of the support.

I have the good problem of having too many lovely humans in my life to list them all here, but I want to call out a few:

My parents, thank you for your love and endless cheers — and for skipping over the pages I tell you to.

Frank and Kilroy, you both mean the world to me, and I honestly wouldn't be a sane person without you.

Bash, my beta reader and Queen B, I owe you one-thousand trampoline class jumps in gratitude for being the ultimate typo-catcher and an even better friend.

Kelly, your design eye is unmatched in this world, and I consider myself lucky enough to have seen you evolve over the years and grow even more into your talent. Thank you for taking my insane cereal idea and turning it into something awesome — and hopefully, purging out all of the awkward middle school memories that we both want to forget.

Taylor, my editor, who is as graceful with her words as she is ruthless with her kindness and patience. I'm so grateful for the time you spend getting lost in this weird world with me — whether trying to go uphill on a bike after getting yelled at by old women, strolling for desserts in the East Village, laughing hysterically in Franklin Hall, or between the pages of this book.

Grant, my husband, essentially made this book possible. He has forever encouraged me to chase my dreams and is my biggest supporter and first reader. When I sat down to write this book, he lovingly replenished my snack options and checked in without disrupting the fuzzy world of my own mind that I'd sunk into. Because of him, I wrote the big, scary first draft in eight days (yeah, really), and I'm ridiculously grateful for him. I love you.

Irene. If you noticed at the beginning, this work is dedicated to her. Although she died before she got the chance to read any of my books, if I'm feeling any sort of emotion wholly (happiness or sadness or anything in between) and can't keep it in check, I think of her words, her infectious laugh, her stories, her red hair, and her little blue car, and it gives me a little push to keep going.

Finally, to you, reader. I am as thankful as I am terrified that people can step into the lives of the people who crawl out of my brain — and I am deeply humbled and thankful that you've taken a chance on this book.

ABOUT THE AUTHOR

Jennifer Ann Shore is a writer based in Seattle.

Jennifer's career in journalism, marketing, and book publishing spans more than ten years, and she has won numerous awards for her work.

Her debut novel, "New Wave," a young adult dystopian, released in August 2018. "The Extended Summer of Anna and Jeremy" is her second book.

Be sure to visit her website (https://www. jenniferannshore.com) and follow her on Twitter (@JenniferAShore), Instagram (@shorely), or your preferred social media channel to stay in touch.